Life in the Sea

People and the Sea

Pam Walker and
Elaine Wood

Facts On File, Inc.

People and the Sea

Facts On File, Inc.
132 West 31st Street
New York NY 10001

Library of Congress Cataloging-in-Publication Data
Walker, Pam, 1958–
People and the Sea/ Pam Walker and Elaine Wood.
p. cm. — (Life in the sea)
Includes bibliographical references and index.
ISBN 0-8160-5706-0 (hardcover)
1. Marine pollution—Juvenile literature.
2. Oceanography—Juvenile literature. I. Wood, Elaine, 1950–II. Title.
GC1090.W35 2005
333.91'64—dc22 2004024229

Text and cover design by Dorothy M. Preston
Illustrations by Dale Williams, Sholto Ainslie, and Dale Dyer

Printed in the United States of America

VB FOF 10 9 8 7 6 5 4 3 2 1

This book is printed on acid-free paper.

Contents

Preface

Life first appeared on Earth in the oceans, about 3.5 billion years ago. Today these immense bodies of water still hold the greatest diversity of living things on the planet. The sheer size and wealth of the oceans are startling. They cover two-thirds of the Earth's surface and make up the largest habitat in this solar system. This immense underwater world is a fascinating realm that captures the imaginations of people everywhere.

Even though the sea is a powerful and immense system, people love it. Nationwide, more than half of the population lives near one of the coasts, and the popularity of the seashore as a home or place of recreation continues to grow. Increasing interest in the sea environment and the singular organisms it conceals is swelling the ranks of marine aquarium hobbyists, scuba divers, and deep-sea fishermen. In schools and universities across the United States, marine science is working its way into the science curriculum as one of the foundation sciences.

The purpose of this book is to foster the natural fascination that people feel for the ocean and its living things. As a part of the set entitled Life in the Sea, this book aims to give readers a glimpse of some of the wonders of life that are hidden beneath the waves and to raise awareness of the relationships that people around the world have with the ocean.

This book also presents an opportunity to consider the ways that humans affect the oceans. At no time in the past have world citizens been so poised to impact the future of the planet. Once considered an endless and resilient resource, the ocean is now being recognized as a fragile system in danger of overuse and neglect. As knowledge and understanding about the ocean's importance grow, citizens all over the world can participate in positively changing the ways that life on land interacts with life in the sea.

Acknowledgments

This opportunity to study and research ocean life has reminded both of us of our past love affairs with the sea. Like many families, ours took annual summer jaunts to the beach, where we took our earliest gulps of salt water and fingered our first sand dollars. As sea-loving children, both of us grew into young women who aspired to be marine biologists, dreaming of exciting careers spent nursing wounded seals, surveying the dark abyss, or discovering previously unknown species. After years of teaching school, these dreams gave way to the reality that we did not get to spend as much time in the oceans as we had hoped. But time and distance never diminished our love and respect for it.

We are thrilled to have the chance to use our own experiences and appreciation of the sea as platforms from which to develop these books on ocean life. Our thanks go to Frank K. Darmstadt, executive editor at Facts On File, for this enjoyable opportunity. He has guided us through the process with patience, which we greatly appreciate. Frank's skills are responsible for the book's tone and focus. Our appreciation also goes to Katy Barnhart for her copyediting expertise.

Special notes of appreciation go to several individuals whose expertise made this book possible. Audrey McGhee proofread and corrected pages at all times of the day or night. Diane Kit Moser, Ray Spangenburg, and Bobbi McCutcheon, successful and seasoned authors, mentored us on techniques for finding appropriate photographs. We appreciate the help of these generous and talented people.

Introduction

The oceans have always been the Earth's biggest, deepest, and most mysterious treasure chest. Since the earliest humans have existed, people have depended on the seas. *People and the Sea,* one book in the Life in the Sea set, examines the past and present relationships between humans and the ocean. The text focuses on the negative impacts of humans on the physical ocean and its inhabitants. Chapter 1 looks at some of the problems that result from the influx of nitrogen and other nutrients into the oceans. Nitrogen compounds are normally found on the Earth, but excessive levels of this nutrient make their way into the ocean. One primary source of oceanic nitrogen is fertilizer applied to agricultural fields. Rains wash the chemical into rivers and creeks that eventually lead to the ocean. Nitrogen also enters the ocean through an atmospheric route provided by the combustion of fossil fuels. In addition, the breakdown products of sewage systems all over the world drain into the ocean. The consequences of nutrient pollution are complex and can lead to disasters such as the dead zone that occurs in the Gulf of Mexico each summer.

The origins and consequences of oil, heavy metals, pesticides, and radioactive materials as pollutants are examined in chapter 2. Oil finds its way into the ocean from spills, such as wrecks of supertankers or explosions of undersea oil wells, from runoff, and from normal shipping activities. The effects of oil vary, depending on type, location, and amount, but all marine organisms are negatively impacted by oil, and most are killed with heavy oiling. Birds and mammals suffer from hypothermia because oil damages their water-proofing systems. All animals that ingest oil are harmed by it. Heavy metals, often the by-products of industry, never degrade and become a permanent part of the sediments. Pesticides cause varying degrees of damage to living things, depending on their chemical composition and concentration. DDT, a pesticide produced in the 1950s, is still present in the marine environment because it degrades very slowly. Radioactive materials that enter the ocean most often originate from nuclear power and nuclear weapon plants.

The oceans have always been sources of food, and fisheries are the topic of chapter 3, Fishing and the Mariculture Industry. Because seafood is a good source of protein and has many health benefits, it has grown in popularity over the last century. To meet the demands of fish-hungry consumers, commercial fishermen constantly refine the technology of their trade. As a result, overfishing has depleted the stocks of many species to the point of commercial extinction. In other cases, populations of fish are reduced to levels that require governmental protection. Salmon, anchovies, red drums, and large game fish are just a few of the species whose numbers are critically low. Fish that are top predators, like sharks and swordfish, are especially sensitive to intense fishing because they have slow reproductive rates.

Chapter 4, Human-Induced Ocean and Climate Changes, delves into the ocean's response to pollutants in the atmosphere. The ocean and atmosphere connect with one another at the sea surface, where they exchange gases and heat. Changes in the ocean affect global climate; conversely, changes in climate impact ocean ecosystems. The impetus behind most present-day ocean and atmosphere changes is human activity, especially the burning of fossil fuels. Global warming, ozone depletion, and increased ocean water temperatures are some of the most serious threats to the natural weather systems. El Niño, a normal disruption in the seasonal events in the Pacific Ocean, has worsened in the last century due to climatic changes. The effects of intense El Niño events impact ocean ecosystems.

Chapter 5, Endangered Marine Life, focuses on the loss of species and biodiversity in the ocean. The health of an ecosystem is reflected in its biodiversity. Extinctions, which lead to loss of biodiversity, occur for many reasons, including exploitation by humans. In the past, fishing and hunting have seriously depleted populations of birds, fish, reptiles, and mammals in the marine environment. These populations are also stressed by pollution, global climate change, and loss of habitat. The Endangered Species Act is the most powerful piece of legislation in the United States for protecting organisms from danger of extinction. When small populations of endangered animals can be found, they are given protection and an opportunity to rebuild their numbers.

The sea is a wealth of living and nonliving resources. Some of the nonliving marine bounty includes minerals, petroleum, building materials, water, energy, and chemicals, the topics of chapter 6. Freshwater can be removed from seawater by distillation and reverse osmosis, two processes that are relatively expensive, but necessary in regions where freshwater supplies are sparse. Marine sediments are as rich in minerals as those on land and offer attractive alternatives to miners whose terrestrial supplies are running low. With the ongoing worldwide shortage of fossil fuels, the energy of ocean wind, waves, tides, and heat is being harnessed in a few coastal countries. Many of the living things in the ocean, especially those in unique environments like coral reefs and deep sea hydrothermal vents, are proving to be sources of chemicals that can be used to treat a variety of diseases, including cancer.

Chapter 7 looks toward the discoveries that marine scientists feel are just around the corner. Because the ocean is such a different environment than land, it holds chemicals, minerals, and organisms that cannot be found in terrestrial environments. Among these, researchers hope to discover treatments for diseases like HIV and malaria. Some of the most recent ocean discoveries have led to better understanding of fiber optics and multiple lens systems, concepts that scientists may be able to translate to technological uses.

Only by caring about, and for, the oceans can the opportunities for exciting future discoveries exist. In the past, a lot of mistakes have been made in managing the ocean's resources. Much of the work of today's marine scientists is aimed at learning from those past errors. Everyone can participate in remediating damage already done, but more important, each person has the opportunity to be involved in protecting the future of the oceans. In order for the relationships of people and the seas to be exciting and fulfilling, today's decisions and actions must be wise and well thought out.

1

Marine Nutrient Enrichment

Of all the Earth's natural resources, water may be the most essential for life. The Earth's finite supply of water constantly cycles through the environment. Detailed in Figure 1.1, the forces that fuel these cycles are as ancient as the Earth itself. As water travels, humans interact with it on several levels. The ways in which people manage water have changed as populations have increased, often resulting in activities that interfere with the water cycle and upset the natural balance of the system.

When humans were a young species with small populations, their activities no more altered or damaged the water cycle than those of other kinds of animals. For the early hunters and gatherers, waste disposal was not an issue because their nomadic lifestyles enabled them to leave wastes behind when they moved to new hunting grounds. As populations grew and cities developed, people began forming groups that stayed in one place, and the issues of clean water and waste disposal required more attention.

As they developed, different civilizations employed a variety of *sewage* management techniques, most of which were relatively simple. Some of the earliest sewers were simply gutters dug in streets where residents emptied buckets of urine and feces. From the gutters, the sewage flowed into the closest waterway, whether it be a creek, river, estuary, or ocean. This practice was acceptable at the time because conventional wisdom held that running water had a natural way of purifying itself. When the volume of sewage is small, this is true.

By the early 20th century, the quantity of sewage being channeled into bodies of water was so large that it overwhelmed the ability of natural systems to break down and disperse waste. As a result, sewage began to accumulate in local

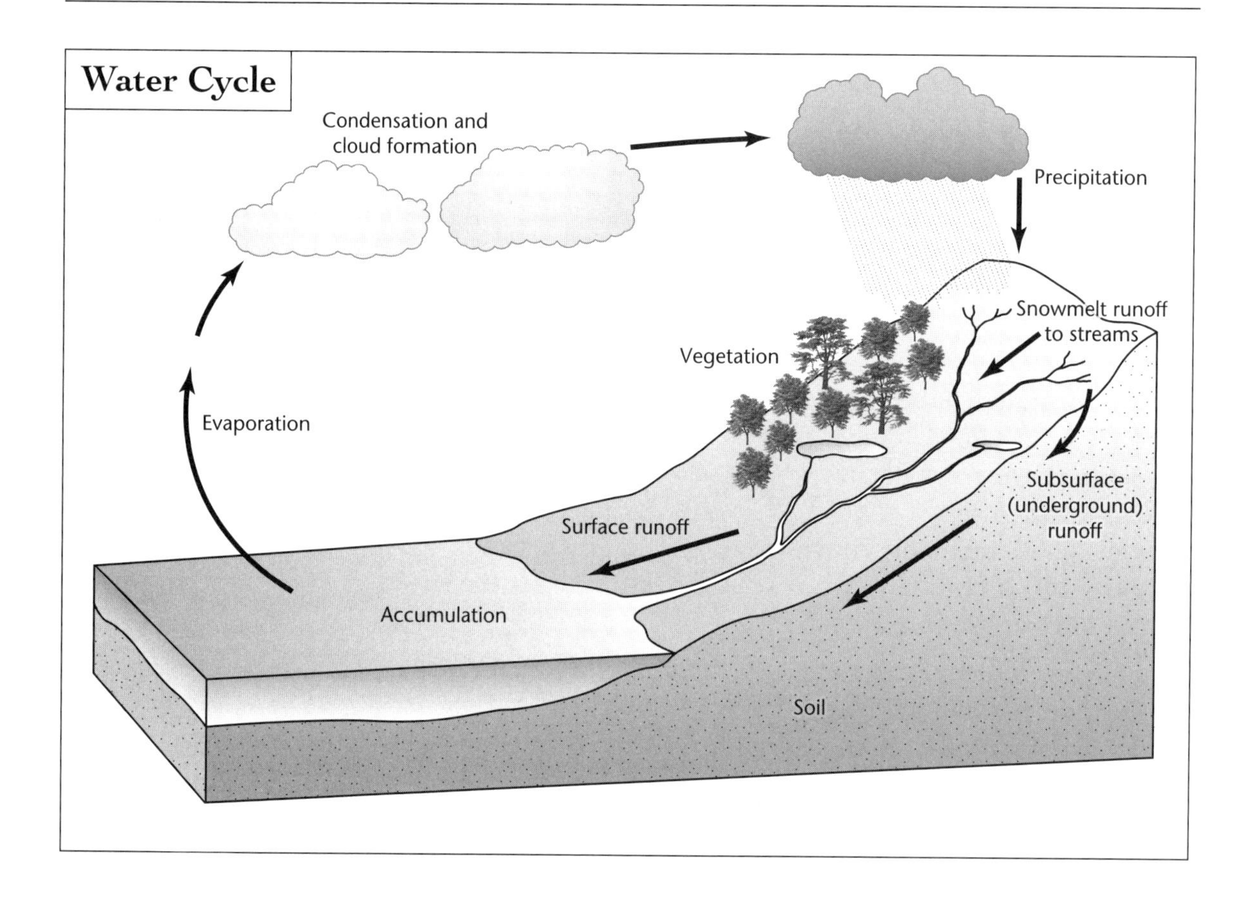

Fig. 1.1 Water moves from one part of the Earth to another in a cycle. After evaporating from the sea and land, water condenses in the air to form clouds that produce rain. Much of the rain that falls on the continents returns to the ocean as surface or subsurface runoff.

waterways, killing the natural inhabitants, causing disease, and ruining water supplies. Added to the traditional forms of community wastes were the by-products created by the chemical processes of early industries. By mid-century, water pollution in the United States, as well as in most other countries, was a national problem.

Laws to Protect the Marine Environment

Since that time, progress has been made. The first giant step in cleaning America's waterways came in the form of the Federal Water Pollution Control Act, or Clean Water Act (CWA). Originally enacted in 1948, the act was extensively revised by amendments in 1972. In the early years of CWA implementation, efforts were directed at point source pollution, wastes discharged from pipes and other discrete points. The act gave the Environmental Protection Agency (EPA) authority to establish and enforce standards for treatment of wastewater, and it funded the construction of sewage treatment plants. Amendments made in 1987 addressed the origins of nonpoint source pollution, that which arises from regions, such as the runoff from farms, city streets, and forests.

The CWA requires states along the coast to monitor the quality of their coastal waters to avoid problems of marine water pollution. The act also enables the EPA to commission research that will help determine the effects of discharged pollutants on marine life and coastal ecosystems, and to use this research to set standards for future discharges. In addition, the CWA regulates factors such as the amount of storm water that runs into the ocean and the volume of oil at sea.

Perhaps one of the most important provisions of the CWA gives the EPA the authority to establish watershed management plans for estuaries and coastal waters. A watershed is the land area drained by a body of water, usually a river. Watersheds vary in size and complexity from creeks that drain only a few acres of land to the Mississippi River system, a network of waterways that channels water from 40 states to the Gulf of Mexico.

The CWA also regulates marine dredging and the dumping of dredged materials. Dredging, mechanically digging up the seafloor, may be done for several reasons. Often, sediment that builds up in harbors and canals makes these waterways shallow and reduces their accessibility to boats. By dredging, boat traffic can be restored. Dredging is also done for new construction, such as building marinas and piers, and to mine rocks and minerals. In all cases, dredging has negative effects on the marine organisms living on the seafloor and can result in the loss of corals, sea urchins, sea stars, sea grass, sponges, and hundreds of other life forms. Dredging also stirs up sediment in the water, clogging the gills of some organisms and completely burying others.

Although efforts to stop ocean effluence have dramatically impacted the way people interact with marine environments, the oceans are still recipients of billions of gallons of pollution each day. The worst hit areas are along the coasts because these are the regions where land-based pollutants drain into the ocean and where people build homes, harbors, and businesses. As human populations continue to grow and move to the ocean's edge, marine pollution problems worsen.

Nutrient Sources

In many coastal waters, especially those of developed nations, nutrient enrichment is considered to be the number one marine pollution problem. Nutrients are substances that increase the rate of growth of plants and algae. Nutrient enrichment, also known as eutrophication, refers specifically to the addition of nutrients, primarily nitrogen and phosphorus compounds, to waterways. Sources of nutrients in waterways include inadequately treated human and livestock sewage, applications of fertilizers to agricultural fields, lawns, and golf courses, as well as excess nitrogen in the air from human activities that cause air pollution.

Sewage, liquid and solid wastes that include human urine and feces, is a major source of nutrients in the ocean. Nutrients from sewage can be carried into natural waterways by runoff, precipitation that does not sink into the ground. Runoff enters some sewage systems from combined sewage overflows (CSOs), drains and pipes that funnel the water that flows over streets into the sewage collection system. In CSOs, even a moderate rainstorm can overwhelm the capacity of the sewage treatment facility. When this happens, storm water causes sewage to wash directly into streams and rivers, which transport the material to the ocean.

The human population, made up of almost 6.5 billion individuals, produces billions of gallons of sewage on a daily basis, far too much material for nature to break down and absorb. For this reason, sewage treatment is an absolute necessity. Sewage treatment removes impurities from sewage so that the water content in it can be returned to the water cycle. About 99 percent of the volume of sewage is made up of freshwater.

When it is "treated," sewage goes through several processes to reduce its potentially negative impacts on the environment. Treatment kills the germs and reduces the biological oxygen demand (BOD) of the sewage. BOD, one measure of water quality, tells how much oxygen is needed (in parts per million [ppm]) by bacteria and other decomposers to break down the organic matter in the sample over a five-day period. Drinking water should have a BOD of less than 1 ppm, while the BOD of sewage is several hundred ppm.

The methods of sewage treatment vary by municipality, although all facilities share some common characteristics. After trash and grit are removed with screens, sewage flows into large tanks, like those in the upper color insert on page C-1, where the majority of solid material is permitted to settle to the bottom. This solid waste material, or sludge, is removed from the tanks and the watery portion is either discharged into the ocean and other waterways, or retained for secondary treatment. During secondary treatment, the liquid portion of the sewage is piped into tanks that support the growth of oxygen-using, or "good," microorganisms. These good microbes feed on the "bad" ones, the viruses and unwanted bacteria. In many coastal districts, water receives secondary treatment before it is released into the sea.

After both primary and secondary treatment, the water is free of solids and pathogens, but still contains dissolved phosphorus and nitrogen. These two nutrients can be removed in another step, tertiary treatment. Some tertiary treatment includes a final disinfection with ultraviolet light or microfiltration. Each level of treatment is more expensive and time consuming than the previous level.

The volume of sewage produced in the United States is staggering, further complicating its effective treatment. For example, in a 24 hour period, the population of San Diego, California, which includes more than 1 million people, produces 2,000 tons (1,800 metric tons) of feces and 250,000 gallons (946,350 l) of urine. This sewage, along with other liquid wastes, undergoes primary treatment to kill pathogens and remove solids. The effluent, or liquid portion, is mixed with freshwater, then discharged into the ocean by a pipe that runs about 2.48 miles (4 km) offshore.

The sludge produced by sewage treatment often finds its way into the marine environment. Sludge is made up of organic compounds, nutrients, bacteria, viruses, metal compounds, synthetic organic compounds, chemicals, and hundreds of other materials. Before 1998, most municipal sludge met one of three fates: It was burned in an incinerator, buried in a landfill, or dumped in the deep ocean. Since that time, ocean dumping has been severely restricted. Currently, some sludge is being used to augment soil in agriculture, although most of the solid materials is still buried in landfills or incinerated.

Experiences from the past provide opportunities to learn about better ways to handle sewage and waste treatment in the present and future. For example, from the position of hindsight, the negative consequences of dumping wastes into the waters of the New York Bight, an indention in the coastline off the mouth of the Hudson River and just south of Long Island (shown in Figure 1.2), are easy to see. In 1890, New

Fig. 1.2 This map of the New York Bight shows the wide continental shelf off the northeastern coast of the United States. At the edge of the shelf, depth decreases rapidly to the deep seafloor. (Courtesy of Steve Nicklas, NOS, NGS, NOAA Ship Collection)

York City began disposing of its garbage by loading it on a boat and dumping it in the New York Bight. By 1934, so much trash had accumulated in this dump that refuse routinely washed back onto the beaches, fouling the recreational areas and causing a public outcry. To solve the problem of trash floating onto the beaches, legislation was passed that prohibited dumping of materials that float. All other types of wastes could be disposed of there. In the span between 1890 and 1971, more than 49.44 million cubic feet (1.4 million m^3) of waste was dumped into the bight, enough trash and sewage to cover Manhattan Island with a layer that is six stories deep.

By 1987, the continued appearance of trash on the beaches finally prompted officials to close the offshore waste disposal site. New York and some New Jersey cities were issued permits to dump sewage sludge 106 miles (171 km) from shore, a region further out to sea and at the edge of the continental shelf. After sticky balls of sewage began to wash up on east coast beaches, all dumping was outlawed.

Worldwide, as the population continues to grow, so does the amount of sewage and sludge it produces. At this time, most developed countries have some type of environmentally friendly plan for sewage and sludge disposal. Many of the coastal developing nations lack sewage treatment facilities, so they still release raw sewage directly into the ocean.

The effects of sewage on the marine environment vary, depending on the amount of discharge and the size and condition of the water receiving the sewage. Because sewage and runoff contain nutrients, most notably nitrogen, they affect the rate of plant growth. Low levels of nutrient enriched material entering the marine systems have little or no negative impacts. Instead, modest increases in nutrient levels can act like fertilizers, boosting the growth of plants. Serious problems arise when high levels of either sewage or runoff add more nutrients than the marine environment can process.

Nitrogen-containing urea and feces in sewage can wreck havoc on the marine environment. Because nitrogen is an essential element for plant growth, low quantities can limit marine productivity. The presence of moderate amounts of nitrogen makes it possible for plants and one-celled green plankton like diatoms and dinoflagellates to grow rapidly but within normal limits. Large amounts of the nutrient can cause algal blooms, population explosions of tiny plants and one-celled green organisms.

In an algal bloom the rate of plant growth exceeds the ability of grazers like fish to keep the plants under control. Fast-growing cells and plants can spread across the water, crowding out other living things and shading bottom-growing grasses. The two most serious conditions resulting from algal blooms are low oxygen in the water and the production of toxins.

Since plants produce oxygen during photosynthesis, it may seem ironic that large populations of plants can use up all the oxygen in a marine environment. Photosynthesis requires light, so it only occurs during the day. During the day and night, plants and algae carry out another life-supporting process, respiration, which uses oxygen to break down food and produce energy for life. In the daytime, when both respiration and photosynthesis occur, oxygen production balances oxygen consumption. At night, large populations of plants and algae can quickly deplete all the available oxygen.

Lack of oxygen causes the plants and algae to die and sink to the seafloor, where they become food for the resident decomposers, primarily oxygen-dependent bacteria. With so much food suddenly available, bacterial populations soar and quickly consume all the available oxygen in the lower part of the water column and on the seafloor. The lack of oxygen, anoxia, causes the death of slow-moving invertebrates like snails and clams. Mobile animals, such as fish and octopus, move away from the suffocating zone.

Only a few of the more than 1,000 species of one-celled dinoflagellates, like the one in Figure 1.3, are capable of producing toxins. One type of dinoflagellate releases a deadly toxin that causes paralytic shellfish poisoning (PSP). During harmful algal blooms (HABs), also known as red tides, toxin-generating dinoflagellates reproduce rapidly. Shellfish that feed on the dinoflagellates are capable of excreting the toxin, so are not injured by it. However, fish, birds, marine mammals, and humans that consume the shellfish are poisoned. The toxin that causes paralytic shellfish poisoning interferes

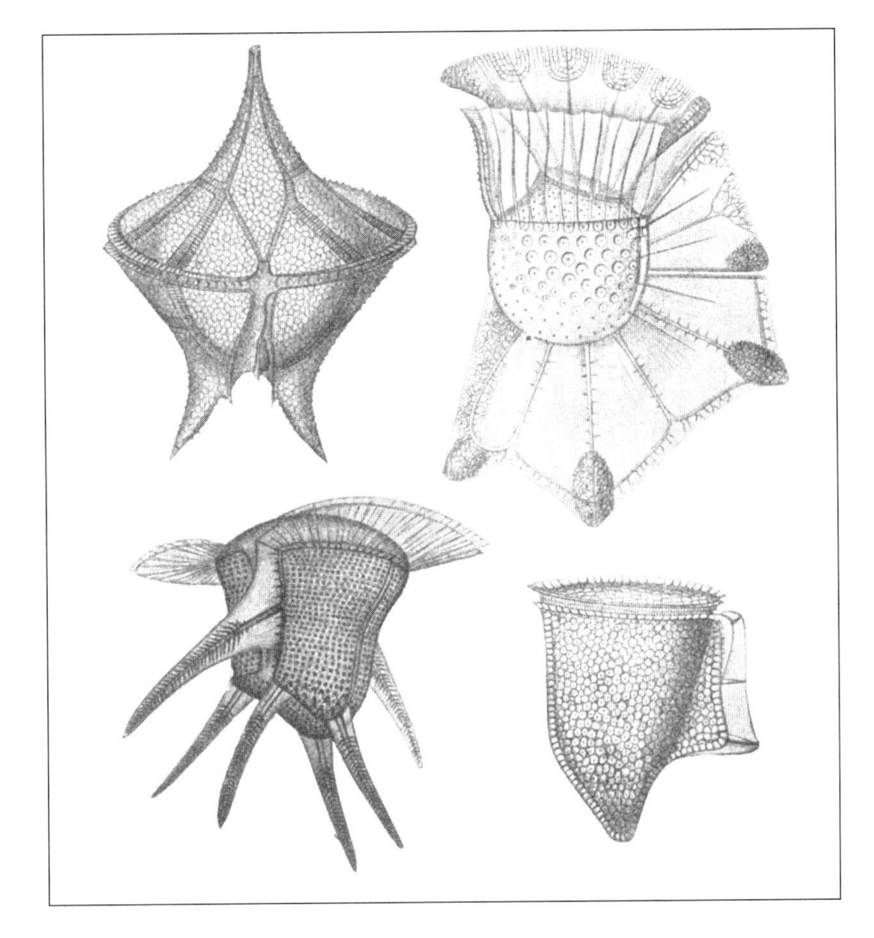

Fig. 1.3 Dinoflagellates are unicellular green organisms whose populations can undergo explosive growth in eutrophic waters. (Courtesy of Carl Chun, NOAA Ship Collection)

with the transmission of nerve signals to muscles, paralyzing them. In extreme cases, death can result. As populations of humans grow along the coasts and eutrophication increases, HABs are becoming more widespread.

Enriched Runoff

Runoff in rural areas picks up the same kinds of nutrients as those found in cities, although the sources of the nutrients are slightly different. In cities, runoff travels over streets polluted with oil products and heavy metals, while rural runoff flows over fields that have been treated with fertilizers and pesticides. Fertilizer contains nitrogen as well as phosphorus, another essential plant nutrient that is often in short supply.

The addition of fertilizer to a body of water enriches the growth of plants there, just as it does on land. Like sewage, nutrient-rich runoff can cause eutrophication of marine environments.

According to the National Oceanic and Atmospheric Administrations (NOAA), symptoms of eutrophication can be found in 138 bays and estuaries around the United States. One-third of those bays are described as suffering from "very eutrophic" conditions. Although eutrophic bays are found on all U.S. coasts, they are concentrated in the mid- and northern Atlantic Ocean and in the Gulf of Mexico. In these bays, about 67 percent of the surface area shows moderate to high degrees of depleted oxygen. NOAA predicts that by 2020, all the currently damaged marine systems will be more severely damaged, and that up to 86 percent of surface area will be low in oxygen due to eutrophication.

Nutrient enrichment also causes damage to unique marine ecosystems like coral reefs and sea grass beds. The input of nutrients into sea grass beds can stimulate the production of heavy grass blades but not an equal amount of growth in grass roots. Consequently, sea grasses become top heavy and lose their hold on the soil. As sea grass populations begin to dwindle, fast growing macroalgae out-compete remaining sea grass plants and take over their niche. Loss of sea grasses, whose roots and rhizomes help hold together soil, causes erosion in the area. Undersea erosion suspends tiny soil particles, making the water cloudy and reducing the number and kinds of organisms that can live there.

In the same way, eutrophication can favor the growth of some undesirable types of macroalgae, which then crowd out more desirable, habitat-enriching species. This scenario occurred in the Baltic Sea, an enclosed body of ocean water located between northeastern Europe and Scandinavia. At one time, the Baltic was populated with lush beds of brown seaweeds and the organisms that graze on them. Eutrophication promoted the growth of heavy stands of fast-growing, green seaweed that had limited use as an animal food or habitat. As a result, populations of brown seaweeds were reduced and many resident animals were unable to survive.

Tropical, reef-building corals are extensively damaged by eutrophication. Corals develop symbiotic relationships with green algae that live in their tissues. Without the algae, corals are unable to build reefs in the clear, nutrient-poor waters of the tropics. When nutrient levels rise in reef waters, algal blooms cover the corals, preventing the symbiotic algae from getting enough sun. As the symbionts become stressed from lack of sunlight, they often abandon the corals, a phenomenon called "bleaching" since the algae are responsible for color in the corals. Bleached corals can recover, but many die. Loss of coral can lead to a change in the entire coral reef habitat,

Nutrient Enrichment in Coral Reefs

Like most other ocean systems, coral reefs are suffering from increased levels of nutrients in their environments. For corals, these higher levels of nutrients are contributing to frequent, and severe, cases of disease. Over the past 20 years, Caribbean coral reefs have endured epidemics that often wipe out up to 60 to 70 percent of the coral populations. Such huge losses change the character of individual reefs forever.

The researchers who made this discovery did so by testing their suspicions about the correlations between nutrients and disease on reefs near Mexico's Yucatan Peninsula. In experiments conducted during 2003, Dr. John Bruno and associates from the University of North Carolina, Chapel Hill, placed various concentrations of time-release fertilizer into bags that they made from pantyhose, then hung the bags a few inches from the corals. The researchers found that even a moderate rise in nutrients increased the occurrence of a fungal disease in the coral known as aspergillosis. Doubling levels of nutrients doubled the severity of the infection and tissue loss.

Damaged reefs rarely, if ever, recover from severe outbreaks of diseases. After the coral animals die, the reefs often become overgrown with algae and macroalgae. Dr. Bruno points out that eutrophication is not the only stressor on coral reefs. Most are also exposed to rising global temperatures, overfishing, damage from severe storms, and silt and sediment in their environment. He emphasizes that of all the stressors adversely affecting coral, high levels of nutrients is one that humans might be able to remedy.

causing many of the fish and invertebrates to look elsewhere for food.

Dead Zones

The consequences of nutrient-enriched waters are far-reaching and complex. One of the worst is the formation of dead zones, large expanses of hypoxic, low-oxygen, or anoxic, oxygen-less, water. The world's second-largest anoxic region is in the Gulf of Mexico, an expanse that averages more than 5,800 square miles (15,000 km^2). In the worst year, the Gulf dead zone has grown as large as 7,728 square miles (20,015 km^2), as big as the states of Connecticut and Rhode Island combined.

The Mississippi River drains more land area than any other river, carrying water from 41 percent of the continental United States. Located within the Mississippi's drainage basin are 47 percent of the rural population and 52 percent of the nation's farms. As farming activities have increased during the last century, the amount of nitrogen traveling down the Mississippi has multiplied by two to seven times.

The dead zone makes its appearance in the spring of each year when the Mississippi River is swollen from frequent spring rains and melted snow and ice. Rainwater that flows over agricultural fields of the productive Midwest picks up dissolved nutrients. In addition, the river and its tributaries carry their normal loads of treated sewage from 40 states. Eventually, the nutrient-laden river water arrives at the ocean, where the less dense freshwater floats on the top of the more dense salt water of the Gulf of Mexico. With the arrival of summer and warm temperatures, the nutrients in the upper layer of water spur the growth of algae, causing blooms. Dense populations of algae use up all the oxygen, sink, then undergo bacterial decomposition, another oxygen-consuming process. By July, all the oxygen in the water is gone, along with living things that depend on oxygen.

Over the past 30 years, the size of the dead zone has grown in direct response to two human practices: the increased use of fertilizer on corn and wheat fields and the rise in number of livestock farms in the Mississippi River drainage basin. Livestock farms produce manure, which is rich in nitrogen. The amount of rainfall also influences the size of the zone because rain carries the nutrients down the river. During a drought in the Midwest in the spring and summer of 1988, only small amounts of rain water were available to wash over the fields and livestock farms. As a result, the anoxic zone was extremely small. In 1993 heavy flooding carried larger than usual loads of nutrients to the Gulf, and the dead zone grew substantially bigger.

So far, the dead zone appears in the spring and recovers in the fall each year. If the Gulf of Mexico follows the patterns established by other marine dead zones, it could become permanent. The general pattern of events is the appearance of a dead zone only once every two or three years at first. After a time, the incident occurs annually, then after several years it evolves into a year-round phenomenon.

The formation of the low-oxygen zone may also explain the increased incidence of HABs in the Gulf of Mexico. The presence of nutrients in the water creates good growing conditions for many kinds of organisms, including those species of algae that cause HABs. As the algae spread quickly, their presence heaps additional stress on the animal life.

The largest dead zone in the world exists in the Baltic Sea, the recipient of sewage from 80 million people in the surrounding coastal cities. Similar zones are located in the New York Bight, the Chesapeake Bay on the eastern coast of the United States, several Scandinavian fjords, the northern Adriatic Sea located off the Mediterranean, the North Sea between the United Kingdom and Scandinavia, and the Black Sea, a body of water that is bordered by the Ukraine on the north and Turkey on the south. In the 1980s, the dead zone in the Black Sea reached its greatest size, covering 7,720 square miles (20,000 km^2). Most of the eutrophication in this region was due to heavy applications of phosphorus-containing fertilizer. When the economy of the region collapsed, farmers were forced to use fertilizer more sparingly, and the anoxic zone began to shrink. In 1996, it was absent for the first time in 23 years.

The far-reaching outcomes of dead zones are still under scrutiny. Researchers know that sessile and slow-moving organisms die as soon as the region becomes anoxic. Mobile animals move away, leaving the region empty of resident life forms. Animals that are capable of flourishing in oxygen-poor environments, like the worm *Capitella capitata,* take advantage of the sudden availability of food and space and rapidly expand their populations. In fact, *Capitella capitata* is so successful in low-oxygen situations that it is used as an indicator species, one whose presence suggests that a certain pollutant or set of conditions is present.

Other long-term effects of the dead zone are complex and difficult to assess. As resident life forms disappear, the food webs change and some native species are permanently lost to the system. When populations of fish vanish, fishermen are forced to travel farther each time they leave the dock. The losses to both commercial and recreational fisheries cause serious damage to the local economy.

Airborne Nitrogen

Although water is the primary transporter of excessive levels of nitrogen to the ocean, the element can also be introduced into ocean waters from air pollution. A high level of atmospheric nitrogen, the product of human activities, was the primary culprit in the formation of dead zones of the North Sea and Baltic Sea. Atmospheric nitrogen pollution can enter the water in two forms: either as dry or wet deposition. Wet deposition includes rain, snow, and fog, while dry deposition refers to nitrogen gas or nitrogen compounds on dust particles.

The algal blooms in the Baltic Sea and North Sea are linked to changes in traditional land uses in nearby terrestrial environments. As swine and poultry industries in the region increase, so does the production of animal wastes. Nitrogen, in the form of ammonia, evaporates from animal wastes and enters the atmosphere. From there, ammonia gas dissolves in the surface layer of sea water or is carried to the sea in precipitation. The same pattern of land use and nitrogen deposition is seen in the mid-Atlantic coastal plain and the neighboring waters off the coast of North Carolina.

Other primary sources of atmospheric nitrogen are human activities that involve the combustion of fossil fuels such as oil, coal, and gasoline. Researchers suspect that the practice of burning fossil fuels is responsible for high levels of nitrogen in unexpected places, like the waters of the Artic and Antarctic, both of which are far from inhabited landmasses and traditional sources of water pollution. Once airborne, air currents can carry nitrogen compounds long distances before they settle to Earth's surface.

While the amount of nitrogen in the atmosphere is a new environmental problem, nitrogen in the atmosphere is not unusual. Nitrogen gas naturally makes up 78 percent of the air, although it exists in a form that cannot be used by most living things. To enter the food chain, atmospheric nitrogen must be taken up by certain kinds of bacteria and algae, a group known as "nitrogen fixers." These organisms use nitrogen in the production of organic compounds within their own bodies. As they assimilate the element, they convert it into compounds that animals and plants can use. Without the process of nitrogen fixation, much of this essential nutrient would be lost to the food chain.

Risk of Disease

Sewage that is inadequately treated can be a source of disease-causing organisms in seawater. According to the CDC, microbes that live in the human intestinal tract, a group that includes bacteria, viruses and parasites, can be transmitted from one person to another through contact with contaminated sewage and through animals like shellfish.

A person who is exposed to disease agents by drinking water or eating shellfish contaminated with sewage may contract gastroenteritis, an infection of the gastrointestinal track, or hepatitis, a disease of the liver. When levels of contamination are high, warnings are posted to let people know. Depending on the severity of infection, symptoms of both gastroenteritis and hepatitis can include vomiting, abdominal pain, diarrhea, and fever. Severe cases of hepatitis can also result in jaundice, a condition that makes the skin look yellow because the liver cannot process bile, a waste product.

Simply exposing the skin to contaminated water by swimming may result in skin infections and rashes.

Studies show that the number of individuals who are adversely affected by sewage-contaminated water depends on the level of pollution, with respiratory and intestinal infections increasing as concentrations of sewage increase. Even swimming in waters that are deemed "acceptable" by the European Union and the United States Environmental Protection Agency is risky. The World Health Organization

Beach Closings

The beach is a favored vacation spot for millions of Americans who enjoy swimming, surfing, digging in the sand, or wading. Each summer, thousands of vacationers are forced to stay out of the water because fecal contamination is high. The problem seems to be worsening; in 2003, there were 18,284 days of beach closures and advisories across the United States, a 51 percent rise from 2002. In Florida, the number of closing and advisory days increased by 128 percent, and those in Mississippi jumped by 337 percent. The dramatic increase in closings from 2002 to 2003 was due to two factors: an increased rate of pollution and better monitoring of water conditions.

Most of the pollution in beach water comes from contaminated storm water runoff and from sewage which carry high levels of the bacteria that live in human and animal wastes. Swimming in waters containing these bacteria can cause vomiting and diarrhea in healthy individuals, and can be life-threatening in infants, the elderly, and people with weak immune systems, such as cancer patients.

According to the Environmental Protection Agency, each year more than 1.2 trillion gallons (4.5 trillion l) of untreated sewage spills into waterways from old sewer systems. Most of the older sewage systems have components that are more than 33 years old, but a few are made of parts that have been in use as long as 200 years. A heavy rain overwhelms these older systems, allowing rainwater and sewage to flow into nearby waterways. The cities strapped with these old systems can be found across the country, but they are concentrated in the Midwest and along the Northeast and West Coasts. The reason that most municipalities have not upgraded their sewer systems is lack of money. Nationally, improvements to sewage systems will cost about $1 trillion.

states that at least one out of every 20 individuals who swims in waters with "acceptable" levels of sewage pollutants will become sick after entering the water just one time.

Animals that live in sewage-polluted marine waters may also be put at risk of disease. In 2001, My Lien Dao, a biologist at the University of South Florida, analyzed tissues from the bodies of manatees, dolphins, and whales that died in the Gulf of Mexico or Tampa Bay. In 11 animals whose deaths could not be attributed to other causes, such as injury by boat propellers or entanglement in nets, Dao found the presence of two microbes that are dangerous human pathogens: microsporidium and cryptosporidium. Both organisms are associated with human sewage. In otherwise healthy humans, the microbes can produce symptoms that include abdominal pain and diarrhea. In immune-compromised individuals, such as AIDS patients, they can lead to serious abdominal disorders. Although Dao's work linking microsporidium and cryptosporidium to marine mammal death is in the early research phase, it is a strong indicator that sewage-borne human pathogens may infect and weaken marine animals.

Sewage in the Ocean

A significant amount of sewage, in both the treated and untreated forms, enters water from oceangoing vessels, with 10 percent coming from the toilets of cruise ships. Large ships operate very much like small towns, generating significant volumes of sewage. At one time, ships were allowed to dump sewage anywhere in the ocean, but the consequences of these practices are leading to tighter restrictions. Currently, the Clean Water Act permits cruise ships to dump sewage and wastewater at a distance of three miles off coast. Many coastal states feel that this is too close to the delicate coastal environments, and they want to raise this limit to 12 miles.

Cruise ships are not the only culprits of sewage dumping; other types of boats are also implicated. Recreational vehicles and other small boats congregate in marinas, harbors, bays and estuaries, all regions that are semi-enclosed. In these sheltered areas, the waters are not flushed as well as those of

Silt and Reduced Freshwater Input

The ecology of many coastal zones is severely compromised by the constant influx of nutrients and bacterial contaminants, but other problems damage their integrity too. In some regions where the influx of freshwater is an important part of the natural ecology, two problems are occurring: an increased input of silt and a reduced input of freshwater.

The amount of freshwater entering the ocean from rivers and streams has a remarkable affect on the salinity of seawater. If human activities upstream reduce the amount of freshwater entering a coastal environment, normal levels of salinity are altered. The construction of dams and pumping stations along rivers are just two of the many factors that divert water away from its natural paths and interfere with the input of freshwater into the sea.

As freshwater input decreases, salinity of the system increases. Salinity affects almost every aspect of marine life. For animals that cannot tolerate fluctuations in salinity, an increase in water salinity creates impossible conditions, driving long-time coastal residents to other, less salty areas and changing the character of the local food web. Many producers such as macroalgae and sea grasses are also sensitive to shifts in the salinity of water and may be less productive when salinity is altered.

Modifications in land use along river systems have changed the normal flow of sediments to coastal waters. Loss of trees, increases in the amount of construction work, and loss of greenways bordering rivers and streams are some of the factors that have contributed to an increased load of silt entering marine environments. Soil that is suspended in water can reduce light penetration to sea grass beds, coral reefs, and other coastal communities. As sediments settle out of water columns, they cover bottom-dwelling organisms and clog the gills of fish and filter-feeders.

Sea grass beds are one of the most biologically productive types of coastal habitats. The habitats created by sea grass provide food and shelter to countless invertebrates like sea stars, clams, shrimp, and crabs, as well as the juveniles of many species of fish. In sea grass beds, young fish are able to hide from predators while find-

the open region of the sea, so pollutants from dumped sewage tend to stay there. In an enclosed waterway, the sewage from one small boat is significant. Studies on bacterial contamination of seawater have shown that the untreated waste discharged by one boat can contain more bacteria than the treated wastewater of a small city.

ing plenty of food. The fibrous roots of sea grasses also protect sediment-dwelling organisms from predators that would dig their prey from the soil.

Sea grass beds modify environments by holding sediments in place and reducing erosion. They also slow strong currents flowing through the region, making the area an easier place for small animals to live. Even the blades of sea grasses provide points of attachment for a variety of organisms, including sponges and algae. More than 100 different species of algae can be found living on the blades of just one species of sea grass.

The health of a sea grass community depends on the amount of sunlight that reaches the plants. Sunlight is not able to penetrate water that is polluted with runoff, which carries silt, pesticides, chemicals, fertilizers, and other pollutants. These pollutants increase the turbidity, or cloudiness, of the water column. Under extreme circumstances, heavy loads of silt can smother sea grass.

Because of pollution, sea grass beds are disappearing in most coastal regions. In the Chesapeake Bay, sea grasses have declined 90 percent from peak levels, and areas of the Gulf of Mexico have dropped off from 20 to 100 percent. Once lost, sea grass beds are slow to recover and may take decades to return to productive levels.

Not all modifications along rivers increase the sediment loads. Construction can decrease the amount of sediment reaching the sea. Damming to control floods or to build power plants can trap sand and gravel that might once have traveled to the ocean, interfering with the natural replacement of sediment that is lost to coastal erosion.

Construction along beaches can also change the natural distribution of coastal materials. Breakwaters and jetties are structures that are often built to prevent the loss of sand on beaches. Once protected by these artificial structures, these sands can no longer be transported down the beach by natural actions of longshore currents, which move parallel to the beach and normally carry sediments from one end of the beach to the other. Such engineering projects preserve sand and soil in one region but cause changes in the normal deposition of sediment in other parts of the beach.

Conclusion

With experience and education, people are learning that the oceans are fragile and subject to damage by activities in the sea and on the land. Research is leading to a better understanding of natural marine systems, and a sense of responsibility to care for and manage those systems.

High levels of nitrogen that enter terrestrial waterways and travel to the seas cause eutrophication. Nitrogen in marine environments is derived from several sources, including sewage, runoff, and the atmosphere. In addition, construction on some rivers has produced heavier-than-normal loads of silt and sediment, while projects on others hold back sediments, preventing them from playing their traditional roles in soil replenishment.

The pollution problems that plague the waters of the Gulf of Mexico are typical of plights of coastal marine systems globally. Rainwater that runs off farms, livestock operations, and lawns carries high levels of nitrogen into the Mississippi. In addition, the river is the ultimate depository of sewage from more than 40 percent of the continental United States. When all this nitrogen-enriched water reaches the Gulf of Mexico in the spring, it floats on top of the salty gulf waters. As the weather warms, these nutrients spur algal blooms.

Nitrogen and phosphorus compounds act like fertilizers, boosting production in both microscopic green organisms and macroalgae. As populations of algae grow, they consume all the available oxygen in the water, then die and sink to the seafloor. There they become food for oxygen-dependent decomposers, whose own populations experience explosive growth. As levels of decomposers climb, oxygen supplies dwindle until the region is eventually anoxic. The resulting dead zone can no longer support oxygen-using organisms, and food webs in the entire region are impacted.

Unless the amounts of nutrients entering the Mississippi River are drastically reduced, the dead zone of the Gulf of Mexico is destined to become a year-round event. To alter this possibility, millions of people in the central United States must work together to reduce nutrient loads in the river system. In addition, wetlands and natural areas must be guarded to protect streams and small rivers that feed the Mississippi River. Eutrophication and anoxia in the Gulf result from planning that only sets short term goals. To put an end to this type of ocean pollution, citizens must shift their focus to long-term planning.

2

Oil, Trash, and Toxic Marine Pollution

Marine degradation is a problem of global scope. For centuries, nearshore waters have been treated as dumping grounds for trash and surplus materials. These same waters receive pollutants from rivers that drain into the ocean. As a result, marine pollutants are more concentrated near the coasts than they are in the open sea.

During beach cleanups, group efforts to physically remove pollutants that wash ashore, the most frequently found item is plastic. Such finds reflect the abundance of this material in the oceans. Many of the other pollutants are invisible or difficult to detect. Oil, heavy metals, pesticides, and radioactive materials are often incorporated in the water column, covered in sediment, or dissolved in the water. Oil is most noticeable when spills release hundreds of thousands of gallons of toxic material into the ocean environment. Sources of polluting oil include oil transport, oil exploration, and normal ship operations.

Oil in the Ocean

Modern civilization runs on oil. Without crude oil, the thick black sludge that comes from inside the Earth, products such as gasoline and diesel fuel would not exist. In most parts of the world, oil products provide the energy to run modern conveniences such as transportation, heat, and electricity.

Oil reserves are not evenly distributed around the planet. More than 65 percent of the stores of oil are located deep under the Earth's crust in the Persian Gulf, with smaller supplies scattered around the globe. The primary consumers of oil, industrialized regions of Europe, North America, and the western Pacific Rim, are not located close to the sources. As a result, oil must be transported from its sources to the consumers. The most common method of moving oil over long distances is in enormous ships called supertankers. Oil can also be piped for relatively short distances. As oil is transferred from one place to another, some of it ends up in the marine environment.

A little oil in the marine environment is normal. Natural hydrocarbon seeps continuously leak low levels of oil into the sea. Excessive amounts of oil in the ocean have complex consequences, many of which are the basis for long-term, negative ecological changes. Some of the problems caused by spilled oil are immediately obvious, like the thousands of dead clams that washed onto a beach in South Carolina after an offshore oil spill, shown in the lower color insert on page C-1. Other problems are more subtle.

The behavior of oil in water is predictable. Oil is lighter than water, so it floats on the surface. Any oil released into the ocean quickly spreads out to form a thin layer, usually about 0.0039 inches (0.1 mm) thick, called a slick. As time passes, the slick continues to spread and eventually forms a sheen, an even thinner layer that gives water a rainbow-like appearance.

Oil harms living things in a variety of ways. The extent of the damage depends on the type and volume of oil involved, as well as the length of time organisms are exposed to it. Microbes, plants, and fungi rarely survive an oiling of any type. Once drenched, these organisms cannot carry out essential life processes such as gas exchange.

Fish are damaged by oil on several levels. The eggs of fish are more vulnerable to injury than adult fish, since eggs easily absorb oil through their delicate membranes. In mature fish, oil coats the gills and interferes with breathing. Oil ingested as fish feed on insects and plants can lead to problems such as reduced growth, damaged fins, and lowered reproductive rates. Fish that are exposed to constant, low levels of oil experience genetic changes and cancer.

Oil can also be a death sentence for sea birds. The feathers of birds are coated with waterproofing body oils to repel moisture. Feathers are arranged so they overlap one another like shingles on a roof, protecting the bodies of birds from wet and cold conditions. The arrangement of feathers, along with the natural avian oil, acts as an effective insulator because it traps a layer of air close to the body that helps the animal retain body heat. When crude or refined oil gets on the feathers, it removes their waterproofing and makes the birds vulnerable to water and cold temperatures. As a result, most birds that experience oiling suffer from hypothermia. In addition, birds preen, or clean, their feathers, an activity that can sicken them because it gets a lot of oil into their bodies. Some birds also ingest oil by eating food that is coated in it.

Mammals that live in cold climates rely on two adaptations to keep them warm. Like birds, mammals have a thick body covering which they meticulously groom with waterproofing oil. The fur of otters is dense, providing them with warm winter coats. As oiled otters and other grooming mammals clean themselves, they swallow a lot of the pollutant. Seals and whales, on the other hand, depend on blubber rather than hair to keep them warm. They get along better during and after an oil spill because they take in less oil than animals that groom. Mammals also ingest the chemical by feeding on oil-covered organisms and suffer irritation of eyes and lungs from evaporation of some compounds in oil.

Oil may be released in the raw, or unprocessed, form or after it has been refined. Raw, or crude, oil is not as dangerous to living things as refined oil. Crude oil breaks down, or degrades, when exposed to the elements. A large quantity of crude oil, 30 to 40 percent, evaporates during the first 24 to 48 hours of a spill. The compounds that evaporate are the most toxic flammable portions of the mix. Most of the components in crude oil do not dissolve in water, so remain out of the food chain and safely isolated from some living things. Eventually the oil in a crude-oil spill is dispersed by seawater, where its dangers are diluted by the enormous volume of the ocean. An area suffering from a crude-oil spill can recover in about five years.

On the other hand, refined oil poses more dangers for living things. The process of refining removes the heavier, less biologically active parts of oil and concentrates the biologically active ones. Many refining processes also add other compounds to refined oil that are toxic to living things. As a result, refined oil stays around longer, and does more damage, than crude oil. Refined oil from a spill on the coast of Massachusetts 30 years ago is still obvious in the sediments of that beach today.

About 37 million gallons (0.88 million barrels) of oil are spilled in the ocean each year. Oil spills are relatively recent environmental problems, coming into existence only after the establishment of large oil fields, supertankers, and pipelines. One of the first major oil spills occurred when the *Torrey Canyon,* a supertanker, wrecked in March of 1967.

Oil Spills

While carrying a full load from the oil fields of Kuwait, the tanker ship *Torrey Canyon,* wrecked off the southern coast of the United Kingdom. The ship's master accidentally steered the ship onto rocks in the Scilly Isles, a group of five islands that lies 28 miles off the southernmost tip of Great Britain. Rocks pierced the hull of the tanker, and 35 million gallons (0.85 million barrels) of crude oil seeped out of the ship. At first, winds blew the oil toward the English coasts of Cornwall and Brittany, two important vacation destinations and key elements of the British tourist industry. Since the world had no previous experience with oil spills, emergency rescue plans did not exist, and no one knew exactly what to do. For 10 days, the British government watched the oil cover beaches and marshes while it debated the best course of action. Eventually officials decided to bomb the tanker in hopes of burning the oil left inside. Once ignited, the blazing crude oil in the ship's hull, along with the oil that had already spread on top of the coastal waters, created a sea of fire for miles in all directions.

The extremely large, intense fire that erupted left much of the oil unburned and the pristine British beaches still threatened. To halt the progress of oil toward land, the government eventually sanctioned the use of detergents and emulsifiers, chemicals designed to break up the oil slick and help it dissipate in the water. Two million gallons (10,000 tons) of chemicals were sprayed on the slick. These chemicals proved to be more toxic to wildlife than the oil itself and caused the death of all of the limpets, barnacles, and plankton in the area.

Diving birds suffered terribly from the spill and the emulsifiers. Officials estimate that more than 25,000 sea birds were badly oiled. More than 8,000 birds were rescued and brought in for care, but in the long run, the efforts proved to be unsuccessful. One month after they were treated, only 450 birds were still alive. These survivors were eventually tagged and released, but only 80 are known to have survived. Birds that were not captured died from shock and hypothermia.

A change in the wind carried part of the oil slick to the beaches of France, but there the results were not quite as disastrous. Because it took longer for the oil to make its way to the French coast, the government had more time to contemplate the best course of action. Scientists, brought in to evaluate the situation and give suggestions, recommended avoiding the use of toxic chemicals, suggesting instead that powdered chalk be sprinkled on the oil slick. The chalk bound the oil into clumps that sank to the bottom and out of the way of many living things.

A different type of oil-carrying vessel wrecked in September of 1969. During the night, a tugboat pulled the *Florida,* an oil barge, toward the power plant on the Cape Cod, Massachusetts, canal. When the towlines broke, the barge went adrift and hit boulders, creating a gash in the hull that released 175,000 gallons (4,167 barrels) of light, refined oil. Winds blew the lightweight oil up the coast for miles. The effects were swift and deadly; poisoned animals, including shellfish, birds, worms, and fish, washed ashore for days.

After the lessons learned from the wreck of the *Torrey Canyon,* scientists were immediately asked for help containing the *Florida* spill. One future-thinking group of scientists began a study of the event that has proved to be instrumental in analyzing the short- and long-term effects of this kind of environmental disaster. That particular study of the oil spill is still ongoing today.

Researchers began their study by trawling the shallow-water bottom of the affected area shortly after the spill to find out how bottom-dwelling plants and animals had fared. The trawl revealed that everything living in the sediment was killed. A few weeks later, a second trawl showed that *Capitella,* a worm that had previously not been abundant in the area, was beginning to fill the void left by the death of other kinds of organisms. Because they are resistant to damage by oil, populations of *Capitella* worms flourished and were soon found everywhere.

Oil lost by the *Florida* continued to move through the region over the next several years. Twelve months after the initial spill, oil was just reaching nearby marshes, wetlands, and tidal flats. These areas suffered the same pattern of destruction as the beaches that were oiled immediately after the spill, losing most of their animal life. Even today, oil is still present in the sediments. Scientists find that by digging a few inches into the soil, they can easily uncover refined oil. In many places, living things have returned to the soil surface, but populations deep in the soils are still undersized.

The first offshore oil well was drilled in the Gulf of Mexico in 1946, leading to a proliferation of productive and exploratory drilling. Oil-drilling rigs used for exploration, like the one in Figure 2.1, are designed to be mobile so that once they have located oil, they can be moved and a permanent rig put in place. In June 1979, an exploratory well suffered a blowout. Two miles (3.22 km) below the water's surface in the Gulf of Mexico, the well known as Ixtoc I began to spew oil directly into the water. A loss of fluids called "drilling muds," which lubricate and cool the drill bits, caused the well to overheat and break open. Oil and gas spewed from the well and ignited, setting the drilling platform on fire. The burning platform fell into the wellhead, blocking the efforts to cap the well and end the spill.

Unlike a tanker that is loaded with a fixed amount of oil, the Ixtoc I churned out crude oil at the rate of 400,000 gallons (9,524 barrels) a day. The spill created a black slick that was 100 miles (160.9 km) long and 50 miles (80.5 km) wide. Oil-spill control experts drilled two relief wells into the sides of the spewing wellhead to relieve the pressure in hopes that workers could get close to the blown wellhead and close it off. At the same time, skimmers, equipment that can remove oil from the water's surface, were brought in to control its spread. The chopping waves and strong winds rendered them largely ineffective.

The relief wells failed, forcing the engineers to try other solutions. More than 100,000 steel and lead balls were injected into the wellhead in an attempt to seal it. This action helped but did not stop the flow. Specialists lowered a hatlike steel cone over the well. The cone also slowed the gushing oil but still did not stop it. In mid-October, four months after the accident, oil was still flowing into the Gulf of Mexico. Finally, cement plugs were used to close the last of the opening. By the time the final plugs were in place, the well had lost about 140 million gallons (3.33 million barrels) of oil.

The damage to sea life was extensive. More than 1,400 birds had oiled feathers or feet. Royal terns, blue-faced boobies, sanderlings, willets, piping plovers, black-bellied plovers, and snowy plovers suffered oiling to their feathers, while great blue herons, black-crowned night herons, noddy terns, cattle egrets, and snowy egrets had tarred feet. In the immediate area of water near the spill, shrimp populations were decimated. By the time the crude oil floated to the Texas coast, it had aged somewhat and begun to lose it toxicity. Even so, the gummy residue threatened the nesting sites of Kemp's ridley sea turtle, an

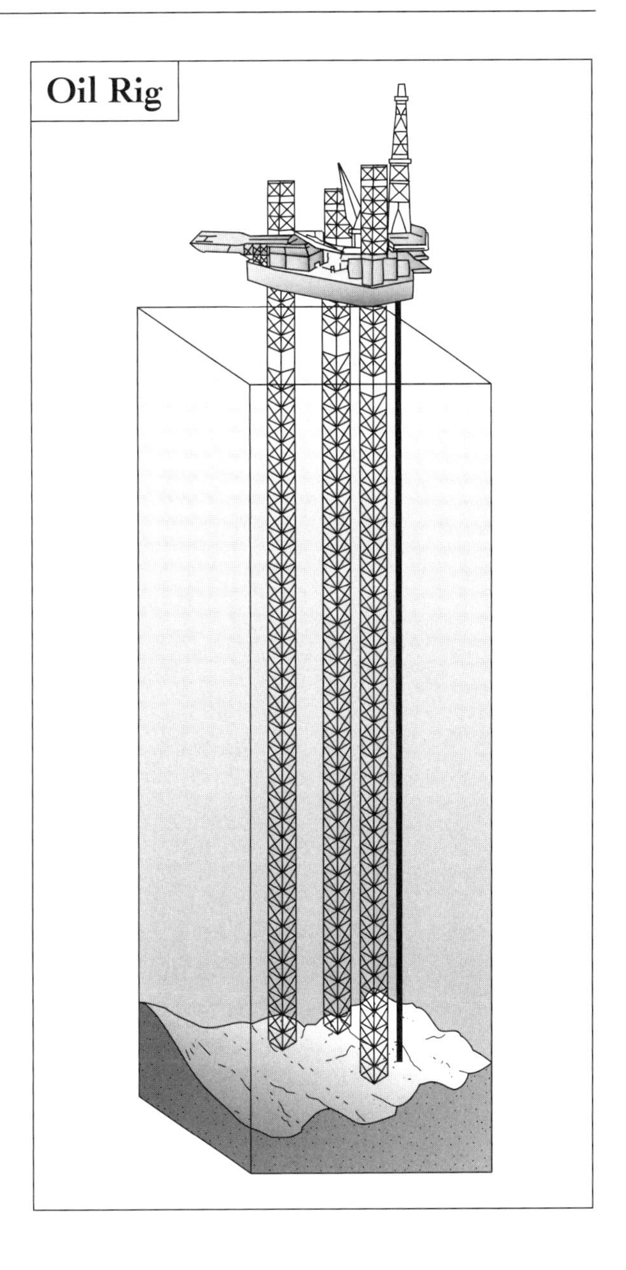

Fig. 2.1 Exploratory offshore oil rigs are mobile structures. After a jack-up rig is floated out to sea and positioned, telescopic legs are extended to the seabed. When drilling is complete, the legs can be retracted and the rig moved to another site.

endangered animal that lays eggs only on a beach in northern Mexico.

Perhaps the most publicized oil spill is the disaster of the supertanker *Exxon Valdez,* the largest spill in the United States. In March of 1989, the *Exxon Valdez* ran aground on shallow rocks in Prince William Sound in Alaska. Immediately, 11 million gallons (0.2619 million barrels) of crude oil began to spread across the water. The oil slick was huge, covering an area that would have extended from the coast of North Carolina to Connecticut if it had occurred off the east coast of the United States.

In response to the wreck, thousands of people flocked to the area to help, some volunteers, some hired by the government, and some by Exxon. Their first goals were to contain the oil so it could not spread further, reduce the loss of animal life, and clean the beaches. Efforts were hampered by rough, chopping waters and cold weather. In addition, the coastline of Prince William Sound is rocky and more difficult to clean than a sandy beach. The death toll was staggering. Volunteers and scientists found millions of dead fish and invertebrates washed up on shore. Estimates of animals killed included 3,000 otters. The number of sea bird fatalities is estimated to be 250,000, and an unknown number of harbor seals and killer whales were injured or killed.

As in the past, some of the cleanup efforts were more damaging than useful. Along the rocky shores, high-pressure, hot water was hosed on the rocks to clean them. As the hot water ran off the rocks and into the sand, it cooked many of the invertebrates that had survived the initial insult of oiling. To this day, the effects of the *Exxon Valdez* spill are still being evaluated.

Recovery in Prince William Sound is very slow. Part of the reason is that many marine animals, like birds and mammals, have very low reproduction rates, even in good years. Sea birds lay only one egg each year, and even under normal circumstances, not every nesting pair lays an egg. In addition, not all the eggs that are laid yield chicks that live to sexual maturity. In the three years following the oil spill, some species of birds had complete reproductive failure.

Otters ingested a lot of toxic oil as they tried to clean themselves. Of the ones captured and cleaned by volunteers, 70 percent died later. Harbor seals were oiled when they swam through contaminated water and climbed onto oil-covered rocks. However, the number of fatalities of seals is not known. When harbor seals die, their bodies sink rather than float. Scientists estimate that their populations dropped to about one-third of the prespill size.

Follow-up studies of Prince William Sound have provided useful information about the best ways to handle oil spills. One study showed that many of the intensive cleanup operations succeeded only in removing the top layer of oil from rocks and sand; beneath the surface, oil still exists. In all, about 20 acres (8.09 ha) of shoreline in Prince William Sound are still covered in oil. Most of the region still contains buried oil, which is more problematic than oil on the surface because it has not been weathered and degraded, so is still biologically toxic. Burrowing animals and severe storms rearrange materials on the beach, often exposing patches of buried oil and introducing them into the ecosystem.

A much smaller spill occurred in January 2001 when the tanker *Jessica* ran aground near the Galápagos archipelago. More than 180,000 gallons (4,286 barrels) leaked out, but most was pushed to open sea, avoiding the Galápagos Islands, the homes of unique iguanas and other sea life. About 370 large animals who were affected by oil were treated. More than 15,000 marine iguanas died. The *Jessica* disaster was a wake-up call to the dangers posed by even a small spill in an environmentally delicate part of the world.

Lessons learned from the oil spills may make it possible for scientists and rescue workers to be more prepared for the next disaster. Now it is known that most of the oil eventually washes away, but some remains on beaches and in sediments for years. In addition, most of the animals that come in contact with oil immediately after a spill can be expected to die. High-energy weather, the kind that whips up winds and waves, makes the spill less damaging than quiet conditions because the energy helps disperse the oil and breaks it down into a less-toxic form. On the other hand, energetic waters render the work of absorbing materials and oil skimmers virtually useless. One very important lesson learned is that some cleanup efforts can be as damaging to the environment as the oil spill itself. In many cases, areas that were not cleaned recovered faster than those that were sprayed with hot water or chemical emulsifiers.

Despite the outcry after each of these disastrous events, oil spills will continue to occur. Knowing this, new technologies are being developed to fight future spills. Bioremediation, the use of microorganisms to remove pollutants, has been used in a few cases. The organic compounds in the oil provide food for the microbes, which change it into harmless compounds. Oil is a complex material, so a variety of different kinds of microbes must be used. The activities of microbes are natural processes and their effects on the environment are less damaging than some other approaches. Other researchers are working on a material made of fine powder from Australian clay. This powder could be sprayed onto an oil spill from an airplane, causing the oil to form clumps that sink to the seafloor, where they are easier to clean up.

Tarballs

Small, dark-colored blobs of oil that wash ashore are remnants of oil spills. Crusty on the outside and soft and sticky on the inside, tarballs have the consistency of cream-filled candy. These tarballs may have traveled to the beach from hundreds of miles away.

After a crude oil spill, oil floats on the ocean surface for several hours, undergoing a series of physical changes. As the oil spreads into a thin slick, wind and waves separate the continuous sheet into smaller patches. The lightest components of the oil evaporate, leaving behind only the heavier compounds. Some of these combine with water to form a mixture that has the texture of chocolate pudding. The action of wind and waves continues to tear at the tar, breaking it into small balls that vary from the size of a dime to as big as a softball.

If a lot of tarballs find their way to shore, they have to be removed manually. In some cases, it is impossible to get small tar out of the sand, and the old sand has to be shoveled up and new sand brought in to replace it. The number and frequency of tarballs on a beach depends on wind patterns, sea currents, and the frequency of oil spills in the area.

Oil Releases

Major oil spills, totaling about 37 million gallons (0.88 million barrels) a year, get a lot of media coverage and help bring the world's attention to the problems that oil can create in a marine environment. However, minor spills and leaks, totaling 363 million gallons (8.64 million barrels) a year, account for much more oil in the marine environment. Oil from roads, parking lots, automobile emissions, leaky gas tanks, and homes eventually makes its way to the ocean through sewage systems. In addition, the routine maintenance of ships, bilge-cleaning, spills while refueling, and accidents while loading and unloading cargoes yield more than 137 million gallons (3.26 million barrels) each year.

All this oil goes largely unnoticed but may be responsible for much more damage than the leaks from tankers or oil wells. Oil entering seawater floats on the surface and becomes part of the thin microlayer. The microlayer is a natural structure, a unique habitat that normally contains minerals as well as organic compounds like proteins and fatty acids that are produced by living things. When organisms die, the oils in their bodies float to this layer before they completely decompose. A microlayer covers the surface of all the world's oceans and contains its own populations of microorganisms, including larval forms of many fish and shellfish.

Chemicals that are soluble in oil, but not in water, tend to collect in the microlayer. Oil, pesticides, heavy metals (lead, copper, mercury, cadmium), dioxins, and other toxic pollutants may be hundreds of time more concentrated in the surface microlayer than in the water just an inch (2.5 cm) below it.

The tiny organisms that inhabit this layer make up the lower levels of marine food chains. Members of both the phytoplankton and zooplankton are residents of the layer, and all are exposed to oil pollutants. Sea birds float in and dive through the top layer, exposing the sensitive tissues of their eyes, noses, and mouths to the oil, and forming a thin coat of oil on their feathers. For many species of fish and invertebrates, eggs float in the microlayer until they hatch. Eggs of these animals are shell-less, protected only by mucus and cell membranes. By damaging the health of animals and reducing the number of eggs that hatch, the oily microlayer has a tremendous impact on populations and the stability of the food chain.

Oil and oil products reach the oceans in a variety of ways. Many cities have combined sewage overflow (CSO) systems that are designed to transport storm water and sewage to a sewage treatment facility. Originally conceived as a way to save money on big-city sewer systems, CSOs have proved to be environmentally expensive. During a rainstorm, most CSOs release both rainwater and sewage overflow into the environment. In this way, gasoline dripped to pavement or oil poured onto soil are able to bypass the sewage treatment facility. Instead, they land in a waterway that will eventually deliver them to the ocean. The volume of oil transported in this manner is significant. A city of 5 million people generates as much oily runoff as the spill of a large oil tanker.

Trash in the Ocean

Each year, 1,100 pounds (500 kg) of plastic are produced for each man, woman, and child in the United States, a total of about 120 million metric tons. Plastic is used to make thousands of items, including parts for automobiles, computers, furniture, and construction. After serving its intended purpose, a small percentage of plastic is recycled, but most is discarded and makes up about 10 percent of the solid waste. Much used plastic is disposed of in landfills, but millions of tons make their way into the oceans. Although plastic poses many environmental problems, its use increases each year.

One of the reasons that plastics are popular and useful is because they are extremely longlasting. From an environmental point, it is this durability that is the worst feature of plastic. The amount of time it takes for the average piece of plastic to degrade is estimated to be 450 years. This means that once plastic is in the environment, it is essentially there to stay.

To determine the long-term trends in the volume of plastic in ocean water, scientists examined preserved plankton samples that have been collected over the last three decades. In this study, plankton came from the shipping lanes between

Scotland and Iceland. Not too surprisingly, scientists found that the amount of plastic in water tripled during that time period.

Most plastic is less dense than water, so it floats. In one survey conducted by Woods Hole Oceanographic Institution in Woods Hole, Massachusetts, to determine how much plastic is floating in the ocean, scientists found that every square mile of the ocean's surface contains about 46,000 pieces of plastic. Among these pieces, scientists identified items such as fishnets, mayonnaise jar lids, diaper liners, cigarette lighters, bags, cups, and ropes. The largest pieces of plastic were nets and fishing lines that stretched for miles. Commonly known as "ghost nets" among seagoing people, these death traps drown thousands of birds, turtles, and marine mammals each year. Scientists also learned that ghost nets wrap around delicate coral reefs, strangling and starving the coral animals, other reef invertebrates, and a variety of reef fish, paving the way for the growth of algae on top of the delicate coral.

Since the 1970s, environmentalists have been gathering data about the negative impacts of plastic in the ocean. Six-pack rings, one of the most troublesome items, form nooses that strangle fish and birds. Sea turtles, mistaking plastic bags and balloons for jellyfish, consume these plastic items, which block the animals' digestive systems and cause them to either choke to death or starve. Some animals, like the Hawaiian monk seal in the upper color insert on page C-2, get plastic ropes wrapped around their necks. Birds, like albatross and gulls, search for red, pink, and brown pieces of plastic floating in the water, and have been found with toothbrushes, toys, cigarette lighters, and jar lids in their stomachs. The albatross in the lower color insert on page C-2 are floating among, and eating, bits of plastic. Apparently the birds mistake these brightly colored chunks of debris for shrimp. Baby seabirds have been found starved to death in their nests, their stomachs packed full of red bits of plastic.

Small pieces of plastic in the marine environment may have as big, or an even greater, impact on the ecology as large pieces. Rice-sized grains of partially broken-down plastic are called nurdles or mermaids' tears. Because these particles look like the eggs of fish or shellfish, zooplankton, the tiny animals that float in the upper layer of the ocean, eat them. When zooplankton are examined under the microscope, their bodies are filled with nurdles. Similar examinations show that the bodies of jellyfish also contain nurdles as well as slightly larger plastic items.

Plastic can interfere with the normal functions of the digestive tracts of living things, but they also create another problem. In the ocean, plastic debris soaks up toxins that are not soluble in water. Plastics floating in the water column may contain up to a million times more toxins than the water itself. Some of the poisons found in plastics include PCB and DDT. In an animal's body, these chemicals seep into tissues, poisoning them. Even if the dose of poison is not lethal, it interprets the normal functioning of the endocrine, reproductive, and immune body systems.

Plastic and other floating trash is not evenly distributed on the ocean's surface. Trash tends to accumulate in areas where two different ocean currents abut and create swirls. The largest of these ocean swirls is called the central gyre, a huge circle of water that travels in a clockwise direction in the North Atlantic Ocean. Much of the gyre is part of the Sargasso Sea, a place where sargassum weeds accumulate and the home to thousands of marine organisms that live on or among the weeds. The sea also serves as a spawning ground for many types of fish.

To solve this ongoing problem, some researchers urge the production of degradable plastics or the use of natural materials that degrade easily. Two types of degradable plastic are biodegradable and photodegradable. Biodegradable plastics are tiny pieces of plastic that are held together in a cornstarch matrix. When the cornstarch breaks down, the plastic falls apart. In several states, including New York, Massachusetts, and Rhode Island, manufacturers are required by law to make six-pack rings of biodegradable plastic. Photodegradable plastic is similar, but it becomes weak and falls apart when exposed to light. In both types of biodegradable material, plastic pieces still enter the water. However, they are not large enough to strangle or choke animals.

Toxic Pollutants

Other materials that enter the ocean from land-based activities include pesticides, heavy metals, and radioactive wastes. Pesticides are a diverse group of chemicals that are designed to repel, kill, or reduce organisms that are considered pests, including weeds, rodents, fungi, and bacteria. One class of chemically related pesticides, the organophosphates, kills by interfering with the transmission of impulses through the nervous systems. Organophosphates were developed in the early 19th century. Some were used in World War II as "nerve gases," but in 1932 their effectiveness as pesticides put them to common use. Organophosphates are very toxic but do not persist for extremely long periods of time in the environment.

Another group of chemically related pesticides are called the organochlorine insecticides. These chemicals, which include DDT, were very popular in the past, but most have been removed from the market. DDT, like others in its chemical family, is not very soluble in water but dissolves easily in fats and oil, so it accumulates in the fatty tissues of animals. Because organochlorines cannot be easily broken down by bacteria, they stay in the environment for long periods. Another problem stems from the fact that DDT and its relatives evaporate easily so they can also enter the ocean through the water cycle. After vaporizing, they can travel in the atmosphere to any place on Earth, then fall into the ocean as precipitation. Organochlorines are not used in United States anymore, but some developing countries still produce and apply them.

In ocean ecosystems, DDT and other polluting chemicals are first taken up by phytoplankton, which are eaten by zooplankton. Zooplankton serve as food for small animals, which are the food of large animals. With each step in the food chain, the amount of DDT ingested and retained in the bodies of organisms increases due to a process called biomagnification. In very low doses, DDT and other pesticides have few negative effects on humans and other animals. By the time DDT reaches top predators like birds and fish, it has often accumulated to toxic doses. Environmentalists first recognized that DDT was causing problems in the 1970s. Brown pelicans normally raise hundreds of thousands of offspring each year, but in 1970 the entire population of adult birds produced only three chicks. Scientists found that the parents were breeding and laying eggs, but the eggs had very thin shells. High levels of DDT resulted in fragile eggs that cracked when the parents attempted to brood them.

Heavy metals, a group of natural, metallic elements which includes lead, cadmium, mercury, arsenic, copper, chromium, selenium and zinc, can also be toxic pollutants. As components of the Earth's crust, they are normal parts of the environment in extremely low concentrations. A few heavy metals, such as copper, selenium, and zinc, are essential in living things in very low quantities but are toxic in higher concentrations.

Many industrial processes concentrate heavy metals. For example, mercury is a by-product of the combustion of coal, the manufacture of pesticides and fungicides, and several mining procedures. Electroplating, the manufacture of plastics, and mining generate high levels of cadmium. Arsenic is used in mining, herbicides, and as a wood preservative.

Since heavy metals do not dissolve, most that make their way to the oceans settle to the bottom where they are fed on by bottom-dwelling fish and invertebrates like oysters and clams. The digestive systems of many species of fish and shellfish are capable of excreting most metals that the animals consume. But two of the metals, cadmium and mercury, cannot be excreted, so these elements accumulate in the bodies of organisms that feed on them. As they move up the food chain, the metals biomagnify and top predators end up with lethal doses in their tissues.

One of the worst cases of heavy-metal biomagnification, illustrated in Figure 2.2, occurred in Japan. From the 1930s

Fig. 2.2 During the 1950s, mercury compounds discharged into Minamata Bay, Japan, were consumed by plankton. Fish ate the plankton, and mammals such as cats and humans consumed the fish, passing the mercury up the food chain. Cats were the first organisms to display severe nervous system disease from consuming mercury. Soon after, humans began to suffer similar symptoms and many died. Children of mothers poisoned by eating the mercury-tainted fish were born with severe deformities.

Mercury's Effect in Japan

Stages in the pollution process

1 Chisso Corporation chemical plant discharges methyl mercury waste into Minamata Bay
2 Methyl mercury taken in by plankton
3 Fish eat plankton; methyl mercury accumulates in fish tissue
4 Fishermen catch fish, an important part of the diet of Minamata's citizens
5 Cats feeding off fish scraps on the dock develop strange behavior, such as turning somersaults; many die
6 Humans suffer severe nervous disease; some die. Babies born with severe deformities

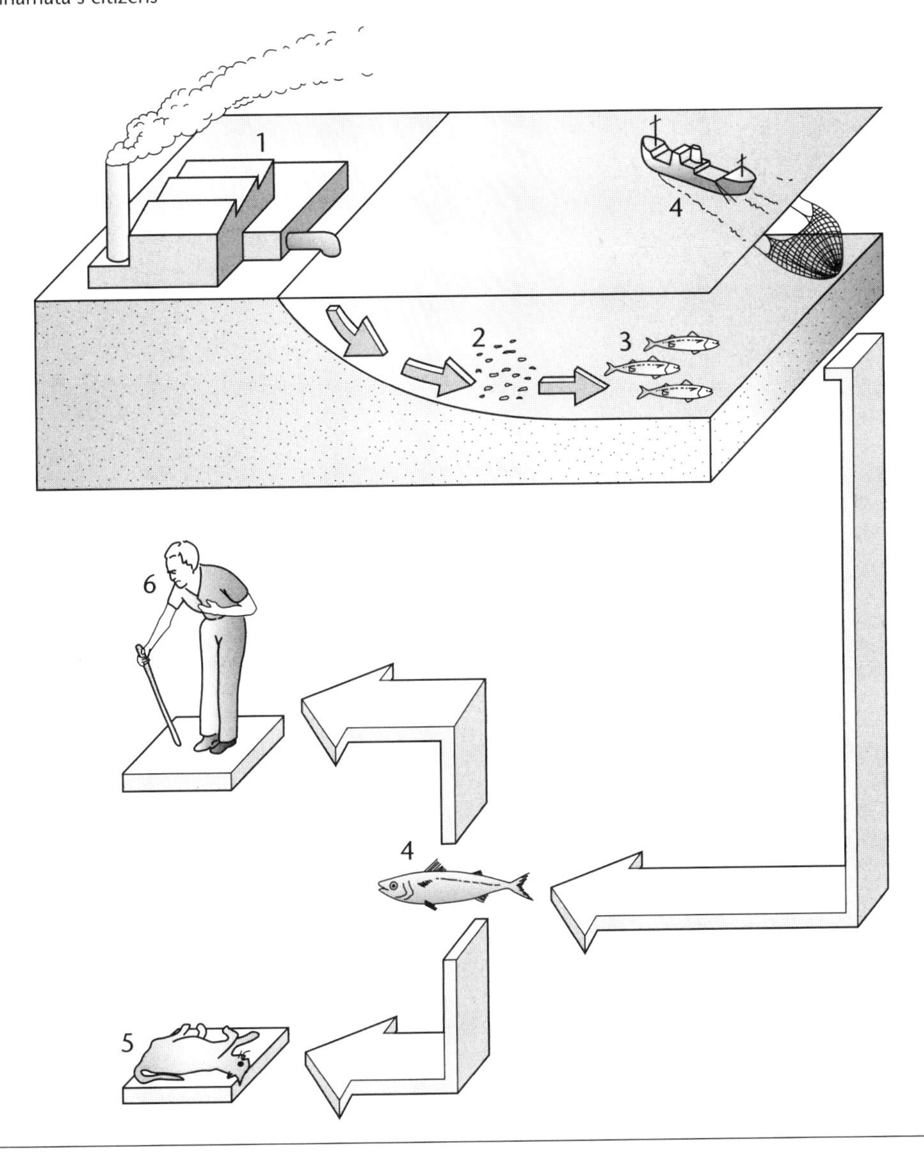

through the 1950s, a vinyl-chloride plant located on Minamata Bay, Japan, dumped mercury-laden industrial waste in the water. Fish and shellfish living in the bay took in the mercury. The safe consumption level of mercury is 0.2 milligrams per week, but people and animals eating fish from the bay were unknowingly getting doses as high as 14 milligrams per week. Since the 1950s, hundreds of people have died from mercury poisoning and hundreds of others have been debilitated with muscle spasms and blurred vision. The babies born to poisoned mothers suffered gnarled limbs and other birth defects. Although the government officially recognizes 2,265 victims, 1,435 of whom are already dead, another 15,000 people claim to be victims of mercury poisoning. New research supports their claims, indicating that even weak concentrations of the deadly metal can lead to birth defects and brain damage.

Radioactive wastes are toxic materials produced when unstable forms of atoms break down. The high energy produced by radioactive decay is dangerous if it strikes DNA, the genetic material in cells. Changes to DNA may lead to cancer and other serious conditions.

Most radioactive material results from the activities of nuclear power plants or the production of nuclear weapons. Waste material created in the manufacturing process is radioactive for 10,000 years after use. Currently, most of this radioactive waste is being stored in pools of cool water, but it is accumulating at a fast rate. Some people have suggested disposing of nuclear wastes in the deep ocean, but studies done on barrels experimentally dropped into the sea show that they break apart. Another idea up for consideration is putting the radioactive waste in deep ocean trenches so they can be recycled into the Earth's hot interior. At the present time, this method of disposal is not being used.

In the environments of nuclear reactors, some dilute radioactive materials, such as weakly radioactive metals, are created in the cooling waters. In the past, some of these materials have entered the ocean. Nuclear energy also made its way into marine environment through radioactive fallout after nuclear explosions.

Some of the radioactive compounds produced by explosions and in reactors are very similar in structure to natural materials that are routinely used in living things. For example, radioactive strontium has a structure very much like calcium, and the body will take it up. Therefore, radioactive strontium can become concentrated in the teeth and bones of living things. Once incorporated in the body, radioactive strontium damages cells and tissues.

The most radioactive organisms on the Earth are marine shrimp (*Gennadas valens*). Found in waters of the North Atlantic that is 1,968.5 to 4,921.3 feet (600 to 1,500 m) deep, these shrimp take up a naturally occurring unstable isotope of polonium, ^{210}Po. Although most of these shrimp contain enough of the radioactive material in their bodies to harm a human, they do not seem to be damaged by it. The shrimp, like many other kinds of animals, are more resistant to the effects of radioactivity than humans.

Conclusion

Damage to the marine environment can be caused by a variety of pollutants, including oil, trash, toxic chemicals, heavy metals, and radioactive wastes. Oil enters waterways in two ways: from accidental spills and from leaks originating from land-based activities. Spills can occur from tankers, oil wells, barges, and oil pipes. One of the most famous oil spills was the wreck of the tanker *Exxon Valdez*, whose hull smashed into rocks off the coast of Prince William Sound of Alaska in 1989. The pristine, rocky Alaskan coast proved to be a difficult one to remediate, and effects of the spill still linger. Thousands of animals died, including fish, birds, and mammals, and thousands of others were injured.

Like most of the recent spills, the area has become part of a long-term study to learn more about the best way to handle future oil spills. One lesson learned from oil disasters is that remediation can be as damaging to the environment as the oil itself. Chemicals that emulsify the oil have proven deadly to living things and efforts to wash rocks and beaches with hot water also cook organisms living in the sand and soil. In some cases, natural recovery is preferable to chemical and mechanical intervention.

Although oil spills have long-term, fatal consequences for many organisms, oil leaks from runoff contribute the majority of oil to the marine environment. Oil that slowly seeps into the sea becomes part of the microlayer, a thin skin of naturally produced chemicals found at the surface of the water. When a microlayer incorporates oil and other chemicals like pesticides, the organisms that live there are constantly exposed to extremely high levels of these pollutants.

Trash in the marine environment has been a problem for decades and may constitute the most obvious form of marine pollution. Plastic is a long-lasting material that can persist in the environment for more than 400 years. Animals living in the ocean must deal with plastic in a variety of ways. Some accidentally ingest large pieces, mistaking them for prey. Others get tangled in plastic lines and nets, often starving or drowning as a result. Small organisms, like phytoplankton and jellyfish, ingest plastic nurdles, taking in toxins like pesticides as they do.

Pesticides, heavy metals, and radioactive wastes also make their way to the oceans from a variety of land-based sources. Some pesticides bio-accumulate, increasing in concentration up the food chain and proving fatal to top-level predators like birds, large fish, and mammals. Pesticides that persist for long periods of time, like DDT, can still be found in marine environments, even though they have not been produced for several decades. Heavy metals never degrade but sometimes are removed from biologically active environments by sinking into the sediments. Radioactive materials are dangerous for thousands of years, and their disposal may be one of the toughest problems facing environmentalists.

Most ocean pollution is the result of short sightedness and lack of planning on the part of humans. The clearest lesson that emerges is that people can, and do, pollute, often because they do not see the advantage of taking care of the marine environment. By gaining a better understanding of the oceans' importance, the world's citizens may also begin to see the advantages of taking care of the resources.

3

Fishing and the Mariculture Industry

The ocean is the world's largest natural resource. Traditionally, the sea has not been considered property, like land, but rather a resource that belongs to all people. For this reason, there have been few restrictions on where and how fisherman could engage in their trade. A simple freedom-of-the-seas doctrine has guided the activities of fishermen for centuries.

When technology made it possible to build far-reaching fleets of ships, questions of sea ownership began to unfold. By the 1960s, efficient fishing vessels were traveling around the world in search of the best catches. Conflicting claims over prime fishing areas led to tensions on an international level. In 1982, after nine years of work, the United Nations produced a treaty, commonly known as the "constitution for the oceans," to regulate activity at sea.

Several important judgments came out of this treaty. One stated that the seabed belongs to everyone, and all people are responsible for protecting it. Another established clear maritime zones called exclusive economic zones (EEZs) giving coastal nation-states the rights to conserve, use, and regulate the resources on their bordering continental shelves. These zones, which average about 200 miles from the shore, provide each coastal nation-state with the rights to its own nearshore fisheries. The constitution made it legal for nation-states to expel foreign fishing boats in their waters. Establishment of EEZs reduced conflict and made fishing safer.

Fish as Food

In some cultures, fish and shellfish have always been the most important forms of protein in the diet. The earliest fishermen reaped relatively small catches using simple spears, hooks, lines, and small handmade nets. The impact of this sustenance fishing had little negative impact on the populations of fish or the environment.

Seafood has historically been more popular in some cultures than others. During the last century, interest in seafood has spread across the globe, and even consumers in countries that previously used very few marine products in their diets joined the seafood marketplace. Two factors accounted for the increase in the sales of fish and shellfish: rapid population growth and new information about the health benefits of eating seafood.

Seafood currently provides 40 percent of the protein consumed in most Asian countries such as Japan, Thailand, and China. The percentage is much smaller in the rest of the world, including the United States, where the average consumer eats only about 16 pounds (7.3 kg) of seafood each year, an amount equal to 6 percent of total dietary protein. Even so, this relatively small intake of fish greatly exceeds consumption in the past.

As the demand for seafood rises, fishermen are becoming increasingly adept at filling it. Today's fishing boats can be outfitted with sonar for finding schools of fish, or satellite links that can show fishermen images of fish schools in the ocean. Modern fishermen also take advantage of hydrophones (microphones that pick up sound underwater) and aerial photographs from flyovers.

The impact of this sophisticated technology on fish catches has been substantial. In 1950, the total world catch was less than 20 million metric tons (mmt). Over the past two decades, the catch has quadrupled, stabilizing at about 87 mmt. While the demand for seafood has risen, consumers are using it in more ways now than they did in 1950, so the proportion of catch dedicated to human consumption has decreased. In 1950, 90 percent of the seafood harvest went to a dinner plate, with only 10 percent as food for animals. By 1980, only 60 percent of the world catch was destined for consumption, with 40 percent used for livestock.

Only a few species of fish are valuable to large-scale, commercial fishermen. The most profitable catches are species of fish that must live in dense populations or travel in schools; species that feed alone are more difficult to catch. Of the thousands of species of fish in the ocean, only 10 groups attract the attention of fishermen. The fish in these 10 groups make up 95 percent of the catch:

Group 1—anchovies, herring, sardines
Group 2—cods, hakes, haddocks
Group 3—jack, mullets, sauries
Group 4—mollusks
Group 5—basses, redfish
Group 6—crustaceans
Group 7—billfishes, bonitos, tuna
Group 8—cutlass fishes, mackerel, snooks
Group 9—flounder, halibuts, soles
Group 10—miscellaneous fish

To catch fish, fishermen must first know where to look for them. Fish are not evenly distributed in the oceans. Since most of the open ocean is low in nutrients, few of the commercially important species can be found there. Most fishermen concentrate their efforts in the two general areas where fish populations are the highest: over the nutrient-rich continental shelves or in areas where nutrients upwell. More than 90 percent of all commercial fishing takes place in temperate continental-shelf water, primarily in the Northwest, Southeast, and West-Central Pacific and Northeast Atlantic. Regions that experience significant upwellings, and attract a lot of fisherman, can be found off the western coast of the United States, western Africa, western South America, Peru, and northern Chile.

Commercial Fishing Techniques

There are several ways to catch fish commercially. Nets and buckets take advantage of the schooling behavior of many species. Traps and baited lines with hooks are some of the techniques employed to catch fish and shellfish that are loners. All the modern fishing techniques are designed to bring in the largest number of fish possible on each expedition.

Hook and line, or longline, gear is a relatively simple setup compared to some of the other fishing techniques. In commercial line fishing, floats support a continuous mainline to which is connected 1,000 to 3,000 secondary, shorter lines, each ending with hooks. The short lines are widely spaced, most about the length of a football field from the line next to it. Hooks can be single barbed or have multiple barbs, and each secondary line carries hundreds or thousands of hooks. A mainline may stretch for 15 to 40 miles (24.1 to 64.4 km). Several types of bait can be placed on the hooks, including live fish, pieces of dead fish, and artificial lures. Some fishermen also ladle chum, ground-up oily fish, into the water to attract fish to the area.

Migratory fish who are top predators in the food chain, like swordfish, tuna, shark, billfish, and halibut, are some of the targets of these longline fishermen. Longlines are strung out in zones where the targeted species are known to frequent, such as the region that extends from the northern coast of South America, through the Caribbean and Gulf of Mexico, and up along the coast of central North America.

Off the central coast of North America, longline fisherman divide the ocean into three fishing zones: the shelf zone, which is nearest the coast; the slope zone, where the shelf drops off to deeper regions; and the waters of the Gulf Stream, a warm-water current flowing up from tropical regions. Some of the most popular spots within these regions are the points where water masses form eddies. Eddies often contain a lot of food for bottom-dwelling fish. A longliner will use weather reports and satellite imaging to find the exact locations of these moving eddies and set his lines there. Places where warm waters eddy toward the shore are particularly rich in fish.

Longline fishermen point out that, compared to other fishing styles, they take in a much smaller percentage of bycatch, or unintended catch. By setting hooks and lines far from one another, fishermen are often able to release bycatch into the ocean with little physical damage. In addition, many longline fishermen use relatively small hooks and line that will break to allow some of the largest spawning stocks of fish to get away.

Despite these advantages, critics of longlines point out that they are responsible for the unnecessary loss of animal life. Some of the animals that are attracted to baited hooks of longlines include seabirds, turtles, fish, and mammals. When albatross spot the baited hooks, they dive for them, swallowing the hooks in the process. Currently, longline fishing is the greatest threat to the survival of albatross and terns. About 400 albatross die each week because of longlines.

Instead of lines and hooks many fisheries depend on active entrapment gear, which includes trawls, dredges, and seines, illustrated in Figure 3.1. Trawls, big nets that are pulled behind boats, can be performed on the water's surface, in midwater, or along the bottom, depending on the kind of fish targeted. In any case, the bottom net of the trawl is held down with weights and the top is held up in the water with floats. A spreading device keeps the mouth of the trawl net open.

Trawls are very efficient at catching species of silver trevally, tiger flathead, redfish, john dory, sharks, and rays, as well as mollusks and crustaceans. On the other hand, trawls also bring up a large bycatch, like the one in the upper color insert on page C-3. In the Gulf of Mexico, where shrimping is a $400 million industry, shrimp trawlers catch finfish such as red snapper and king mackerel as well as corals, other invertebrates, and sea turtles. The lower color insert on page C-3 shows a sea turtle that was trapped in a trawling net and drowned.

Bottom trawling can be done in the relatively shallow waters of the continental shelves, at depths of 328.1 to 656.2 feet (100 to 200 m) or in deeper, oceanic seas. Critics of the fishing technique point out that bottom trawling destroys entire benthic habitats, such as coral reefs and sponge beds. In recent years, interest in fish such as orange roughy has increased the rate of bottom trawling done around seamounts, underwater mountains that are rich in sea life.

Dredges, boxlike devices with rigid frameworks, work very much like bottom trawls. Dredges drag heavy chains through soft mud and sediment, targeting bivalves like mussels, clams, scallops, and oysters. Critics complain that dredging is one of the most harmful fishing practices because, like bottom trawls, dredges disturb the integrity of the seafloor, often

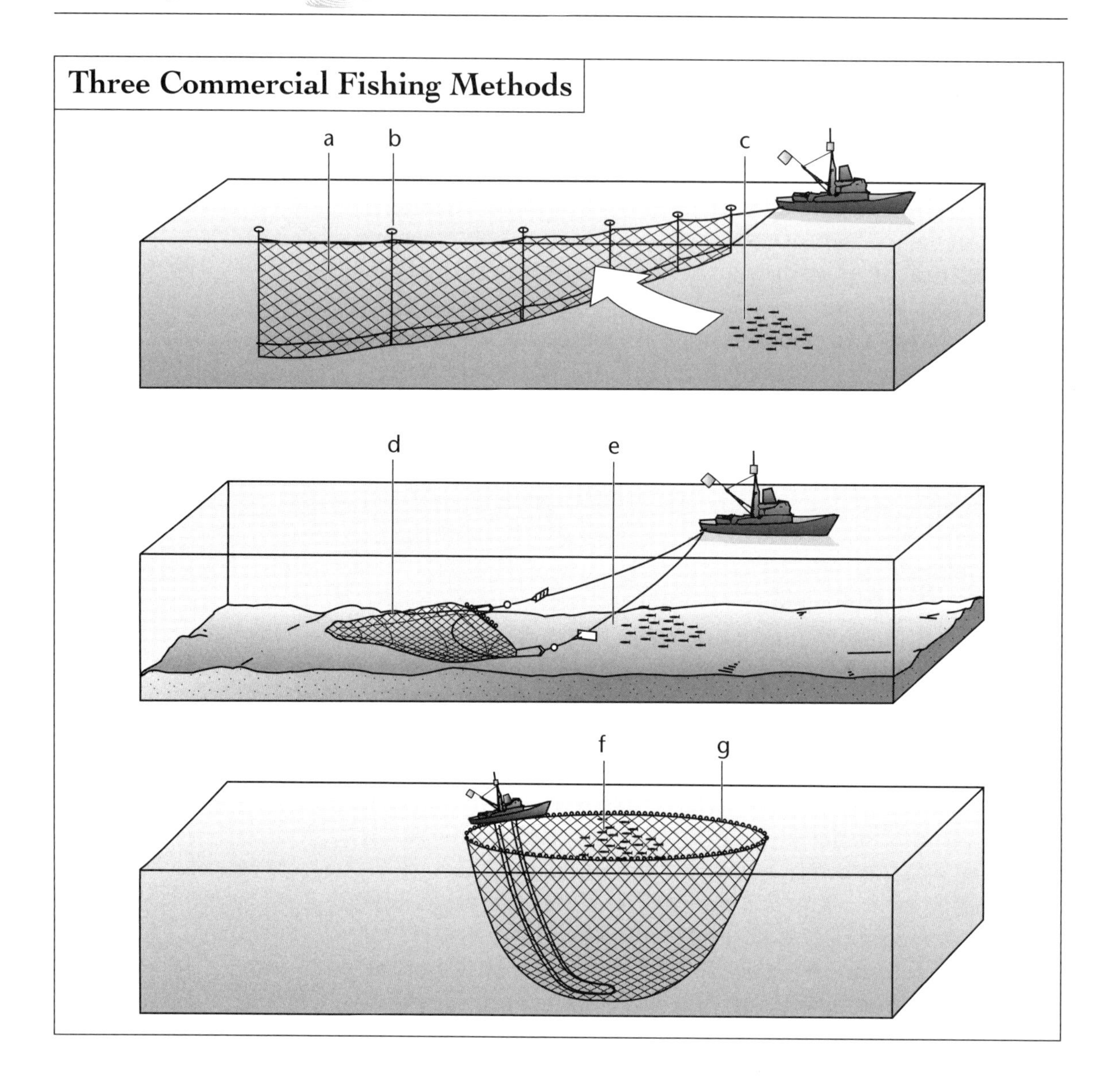

Fig. 3.1 Three commercial fishing methods are drift netting, trawling, and purse seining. A series of drift nets (a) are hung vertically in the water using floats (b). Schools of fish (c) swim into the netting and become trapped. Trawls (d) are large, conical nets pulled behind fishing vessels. Schools of fish (e) swim directly into the nets. When a school of fish is spotted (f), a speedboat can leave a fishing vessel, surround the school with a purse seine net, then return to the vessel. The net can be drawn together at the bottom to create a bowl-shaped enclosure (g).

gouging several inches into the sediments. Dredge gear crushes benthic organisms and damages breeding and feeding grounds of many species. Some parts of the seafloor are dredged hundreds of times a year and currently resemble bare concrete. It can take hundreds of years for the seafloor to recover from the effects of dredging.

Fish can also be caught in purse seines, huge, rectangular nets that are held in position by floats along the top and weights at the bottom. Fisherman find a school of fish, then send one man out from a large fishing vessel in a skiff. The skiff carries the purse seine net in a circle around the school and then ends back at the big vessel, as pictured in the upper color insert on page C-4. Seine nets are 3,600 feet (1,100 m) long and 595 feet (180 m) wide. When the seine is closed, it draws together like a purse, enclosing thousands of schooling fish such as tuna and menhaden. This sacklike net forms a bottom that keeps fish from escaping and can collect up to 150,000 pounds (68,000 kg) of fish each time. As shown in the lower color insert on page C-4, once pulled out of the water, the catch is dumped into the hold of a ship and carried to market.

Because tuna are schooling fish that sell for an excellent price, they are ideal species for purse seining. However, dolphins often get trapped in the nets intended for tuna and drown. Tuna are schooling fish that like to congregate under floating logs and schools of dolphins. The presence of dolphins in the water is such a reliable indicator of tuna that fishermen watch for the mammals to help them find their intended prey.

In the 1950s fisherman would send out helicopters or small vessels to look for dolphins. Once they were spotted, speedboats were deployed to herd the dolphins, and the tuna beneath them, into a small group. The boats then encircled the school of dolphins and tuna with purse seine nets. Once the net was set in place, the net's bottom was "pursed" to keep tuna from escaping. Since dolphins are air-breathing mammals, those trapped in the net died of asphyxiation. Between 1950 and 1990, more than 6 million dolphins died in purse seine nets. As a result, the populations of dolphins became seriously depleted.

Public outcry forced the fishing industry to look for methods that would reduce dolphin deaths. Techniques such as "backing down," lowering the net to let dolphins swim out, have saved a lot of the mammals. In addition, the installation of Medina Panels, nets with mesh sizes less likely to trap dolphins, also helped. One of the biggest factors in reducing dolphin deaths was the refusal of tuna canners to buy tuna caught by encircling dolphins. Today the number of dolphins killed annually is down to about 2,500, and dolphin populations are recovering.

Nets, pots, and traps are used in a different form of fishing, passive entrapment. Traps and pots are small devices that are baited and then set on the seabed, either individually or in groups. Both pots and traps are cagelike, made of a variety of materials from wood to plastic, and opening in more than one place. Buoys attached to pots and traps help fishermen recover their catches. Pots often have one or more funnel-shaped openings. Lobsters and shrimp are two kinds of crustaceans targeted by pots and traps.

Trap nets are stationary, uncovered nets that are anchored and fixed on stakes. In many coastal regions, trap nets are fashioned from stakes, reeds, branches and strings. Most are designed with several chambers that funnel fish into a removable catch chamber.

Fish that are caught in another type of equipment, entanglement gear, literally get their bodies, fins, or gills tangled in netting, like those in the gill net being hauled aboard a boat in the upper color insert on page C-5. One type of entangling gill net is the drift net. Drift nets, made of fine-gauged threads suspended in the water, snare fish attempting to swim through them. Originally designed by consultants from the United Nations, drift nets were introduced as a method to boost the harvest of small, sustenance fishermen in several Asian countries. Big sections of net, called tans, are about 132 to 165 feet long (40 to 50 m) and 23 feet (7 m) tall. One or two fishermen deploying a drift net could bring in enough fish for their families and to sell.

When commercial fishing fleets began using drift nets, they sewed hundreds of tans together, creating walls of netting that stretched up to 50 miles (80 km). Instead of using threads that biodegrade, commercial enterprises make their nets of nylon and polyester, two synthetic threads that can remain intact for hundreds of years. During the night, boats deployed miles of drift nets into the water to catch a variety of fish, including salmon and squid. Until 1993, fishermen from Taiwan, Korea, and Japan were letting out 30,000 miles (48,000 km) of drift nets every night, enough to encircle the Earth.

Long drift nets quickly gained reputations as "walls of death" because of the number of animals they lethally snared, including a large bycatch. Annually, in the North Pacific, these nets caused the deaths of as many as 15,000 Dall's porpoises, 700,000 seabirds, and countless turtles, sharks, and fish. In addition, as fishermen hauled in their catches, the nets would break, setting free miles of "ghost nets" that drifted around the sea for decades, killing everything they entangled. These large drift nets are now banned worldwide, but poachers still use them illegally in the Pacific Ocean.

Consequences of Overfishing

Modern techniques are extremely effective at catching fish. Numerous marine scientists fear that the efficiency of today's fishing technology is pushing many species to the brink of extinction. In some cases, fisheries have already reached, or exceeded, the maximum sustainable yield (MSY), the most that can be taken without damaging the size of future populations. The National Marine Fisheries Service estimates that 45 percent of commercially important fish species are overfished. Some of these overfished species may have populations that are reduced to as little as 10 percent of their original levels.

Overfishing follows a typical pattern. A species of fish or shellfish gains public interest. In hopes of cashing in on the new market, hundreds of fishermen switch their focus from what they had previously been fishing to the new species. The earliest fishermen to get outfitted for the new species find plenty of fish and turn huge profits. Inspired by this success, other individuals or companies invest in expensive fishing equipment in hopes of similar catches, often spending money in anticipation of the same level of success seen by the first fishermen.

In the beginning, fish are plentiful and harvests are good. In addition, many of the fish caught are the large, older members of the population. After just a few years of great fishing, the situation begins to change. Fishermen find that the average size of fish in the catch drops, so they must take a greater number of fish each year just to keep even. There are no more big individuals in the catches because the largest ones were caught in the first few years. With all the mature fish gone, catches consist primarily of juveniles, most of which have not reached reproductive maturity. In addition, fishermen must travel farther, spend more time, and work harder to bring in the fish they do catch. Within a matter of years, there are so few of the targeted fish left that the slim catches do not justify commercial fishing efforts.

One of the first global lessons in overfishing came in the 1970s, when the anchoveta fisheries collapsed. Anchoveta are small fish that consume phytoplankton. At one time, anchoveta populations off the coast of Peru were dense because that is where deep, nutrient-rich water wells to the surface. The nutrients in the upwelling water support phytoplankton, which in turn support the anchoveta.

In 1950 a product called fishmeal was developed. Made of ground-up anchoveta, fishmeal was marketed as a protein supplement that could be added to the feed of many livestock, including cattle, chickens, and pigs. In the beginning phases of the fishmeal business, demand for the product was slim, so only 7,000 tons of anchoveta were required to fill it. By 1962 demand for fishmeal had increased dramatically, and the fishery yielded 6.5 million tons. In 1970 catches hit record highs of more than 12 million tons, accounting for 22 percent of all the fish caught in the world.

In the years of increasing demand, fishermen and scientists noticed that the size of individual fish being caught was decreasing, the first hint that fishing pressure on this group of animals might be too high. In 1972, after a winter of adverse weather conditions, the catch plummeted to only 2 million tons of anchoveta. Finally, recognizing that overfishing of anchoveta had serious repercussions, the Peruvian government placed restrictions and quotas on fishing. Anchoveta are recovering, but their populations are still small.

Another example of overfishing occurred with the red drum or redfish in the Gulf of Mexico. In this case, a relatively unknown fish became a highly desired species after a Cajun recipe for blackened redfish was introduced to the public in 1980. When consumer interest in the fish escalated, fishermen responded. Boats, outfitted with new purse seines, targeted stocks of red drums. From 1983 to 1986, the commercial catch of red drum doubled.

With so many fishermen after one kind of fish, populations of red drum declined quickly. By 1988, the federal government judged that red drums were overfished and banned their harvest. Today the fish are unavailable to commercial fishermen, although recreational fisherman may pursue them.

Like red drums, salmon moved from a place of relative obscurity to one of prominence when the health benefits of eating fish became widely known. There are five species of wild Alaska salmon that are popular with diners: sockeye, king or Chinook, coho, chum, and pink. All types of salmon spawn in rivers, but mature individuals spend most of their lives in the oceans. Unlike many other species of fish, salmon spawn only one time in their lives. To do so, they swim back to the places where they were born, traveling through coastal zones, estuaries, rivers, and streams to do so. Even before overfishing decimated their numbers, many adult salmon were finding it impossible to make it back to their natal streams because of construction projects in their streams and rivers.

Fishermen in pursuit of salmon take advantage of the fishes' instinct to travel inland in tightly packed schools. As schools of the salmon swim through coastal and estuarine areas, fishermen net them. In many places, intense fishing has reduced populations to dangerously low levels. In an effort to give salmon an opportunity to recover, some coastal regions regulate salmon fishing.

For all species of fish, the consequences of overfishing are complex and far-reaching. When one species of fish becomes extinct, or even suffers from reduced population size, all the organisms in that fish's food chain are affected and undergo adjustments. Organisms that are prey of the overfished species may proliferate and cause problems for other animals or plants in the environment. On the other hand, organisms that feed on the overfished species may die from starvation. The loss of one or two species from a food chain disrupts the entire food chain and interferes with the flow of energy through it.

Mariculture Techniques

With the global increase in demand for seafood, one of the logical solutions has been mariculture, growing marine organisms for food or other products under controlled conditions. Currently, farmed fish and shellfish, like salmon and shrimp, supply one-third of the seafood that people eat. Fish are becoming an increasingly important part of the diet, making mariculture one of the fastest-growing branches of agriculture.

The idea of growing seafood is not new. The Chinese began raising carp 3,500 years ago. Even the Egyptians farmed their own tilapia 2,500 years ago, and oysters have been grown in Japan for more than 2,000 years. Traditionally, most mariculture farms have been small, family-managed businesses that required a lot of labor.

Today some small farms still exist, but the trend is toward large, highly automated operations. Altogether, mariculture accounts for about 15 percent of the world's catch, or about 10 million metric tons (14 million tons) of food. Most of the revenue in mariculture currently comes from fish such as salmon and plaice, shellfish like shrimp, oysters, mussels, abalone, and seaweeds such as kelp.

In Asian countries, there are numerous, long-established mariculture enterprises. The United States, on the other hand, is just getting into the market. Most U.S. mariculture is located in the south, concentrated in the Gulf of Mexico around the mouth of the Mississippi River. Coastal sites in unpolluted waters are ideal locations for raising fish and shellfish, but they can sometimes be difficult to locate. The lack of adequate coastal sites has given rise to an offshore mariculture industry within the EEZ of the United States.

Kelp is brown seaweed that can be commercially grown and harvested on "seaweed" farms. There are several important products derived from kelp, including algin, iodine, and mannitol. These compounds find use in medicine, food, textiles, and printing. In addition, kelp is consumed by some people.

In a mariculture method called rafting, kelp are attached to ropes suspended from rafts. By moving the rafts from place to place along the coast, kelp farmers can keep their crops in areas where pollution is low and water temperature is cool, less than 50°F (10°C). Nitrogen fertilizer is used to augment the natural levels of this nutrient in the water.

In the Gulf of Mexico, several marine animals are grown in mariculture. Shrimp, menhaden, crabs, oysters, spiny lobsters, groupers, snappers, mullet, tuna, and black drum are harvested. The most commercially valuable of these species is shrimp, and menhaden are the second-largest harvest. Too oily to use for human food, menhaden are converted into fish meal and used in animal food.

Oysters can be farmed in their natural habitats in a variety of ways. One method simply places immature oysters in shallow marine water, where the substrate is hard. Although this technique keeps oyster populations centrally located, many of the young bivalves fall prey to crabs. Another technique, shown in Figure 3.2, lifts oysters off the bottom, suspending them in water from floating rafts that are similar to those used in kelp farming. Off-the-bottom culturing techniques have

Fig. 3.2 Oysters and mussels can be grown in mariculture. Free-swimming oyster or mussel larvae can be captured at sea with dangling lines, to which they stick (a). Larvae are grown in seawater tanks (b) until they are large enough to be transferred to sea. Young oysters are attached to vertical poles or ropes (c) in shallow tidal waters to grow.

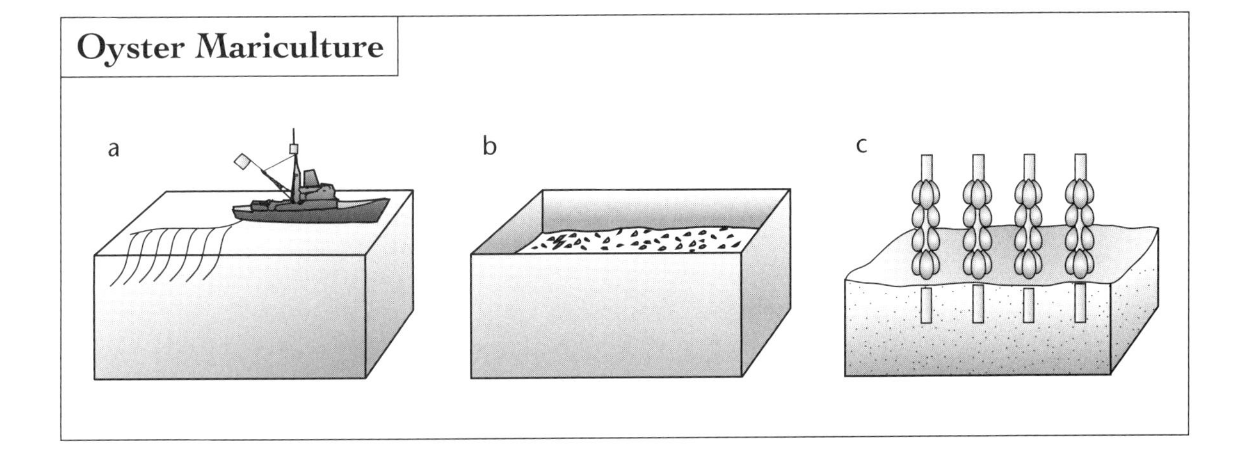

Genetically Engineered Fish

Genetically engineered, or transgenic, salmon are being produced in farms all over the world. One genetically engineered version of the North Atlantic salmon grows seven times faster than the typical salmon. In addition, this fish is more attractive to potential mates than unaltered fish, so it has greater reproductive success.

Transgenic fish, animals that contain genes from more than one organism, are currently being considered for approval by the U.S. Food and Drug Association. A few experimental genetically engineered fish have already been developed for study. Cells of the transgenic Atlantic salmon contain genes from the Chinook salmon that increase the amount of growth hormone they produce. Growth hormone speeds the development of organisms, and in Atlantic salmon it stimulates the fish to grow faster than normal. For farmers, this gene makes fish farming more efficient because it produces more fish with less fish food. Proponents of the project explain that transgenic fish can supply the consumer with a healthy food that was raised and harvested in a way that does not interfere with the recovery of salmon in the natural populations. To prevent the altered fish from breeding with native populations, the developers only use sterile eggs.

Opponents feel that transgenic salmon threaten wild populations. Many point out that if the genetically altered fish were to escape from their pens, they could outcompete native fish in the wild, possibly driving them to extinction. Some fear that a small percentage of the sterile eggs might be reproductively active.

Transgenic salmon are just one of several species of genetically altered fish under development. About two dozen varieties of genetically engineered fish or shellfish are objects of intense research. In most cases, genetic changes are aimed at increasing growth and resistance to disease. Abalone, oysters, striped bass, rainbow trout, catfish, and tilapia are some of the species being used in transgenic fish experiments and research. Other genetically altered species include Atlantic salmon into which have been implanted a gene for cold tolerance, as well as Atlantic salmon that were given a gene from rainbow trout that enhances disease tolerance. Transgenic striped bass contain genes derived from insects that improve their ability to resist disease, and transgenic Indian carps have received a human growth-hormone gene.

been used in Asian countries for more than 50 years and are currently employed in Europe, Australia, and the United

States. Suspended safely in the water, oysters grow twice as fast as they do in the wild, and the meat is a better quality.

Abalones are gastropods, relatives of snails, which are eaten as delicacies in California and Japan. In nature, populations of abalones are small, so the price of each caught animal is very high. Abalone farms primarily sell their wares to restaurants, where they get about $3 for each 3.15 inches (8.2 mm) of animal. Young abalones are usually raised in tanks filled with swirling seawater.

Salmon farming is done in coastal locations all around the United States and Canada. The Atlantic salmon is raised in 85 farms in British Columbia, producing 70,000 metric tons of the fish in 2002. Salmon are carnivores, and on farms they are fed brown pellets that contain 45 percent fishmeal and 25 percent fish oil. In the United States, salmon are very popular, and half the Canadian crop is exported there.

Problems in Mariculture

Although mariculture offers some solutions to augmenting the decreasing supplies of marine species, it is not a perfect answer to the problems caused by overfishing. In many ways, mariculture creates problems that are very similar to those it was designed to solve.

Organisms raised in fish farms must be fed since they cannot forage for their own food. Shrimp and salmon are carnivores, and those in captivity are fed wild caught fish that are processed into fishmeal and fish oil. The quantity of fish caught to sustain salmon and shrimp are almost triple the amount of marketable shrimp and salmon produced. This means that instead of becoming substitutes for fish caught in the wild, farm-raised shrimp and salmon are actually the cause of a substantial degree of fishing.

Pens that hold cultivated fish and shellfish accumulate large volumes of feces, old food, and dead fish underneath them. This nutrient-rich biomass adds to the amount of nitrogen and phosphorus entering the ecosystem. Although the levels of these nutrients from mariculture alone are not enough to cause eutrophication, nutrient loading is collective, and all contributors make a difference. In an analysis of salmon farming in Nordic countries, researchers found that the amount of nitrogen discharged equals the amount in sewage from a city of 3.9 million people. In addition, pesticides and antibiotics needed to maintain the health of the cultivated crop are also discharged into the water.

Some mariculture operations are established at the expense of essential natural habitats. In Thailand, for example, mangrove forests are cut down to set up shrimp ponds. Normally mangrove forests serve as nurseries for young fish and shellfish of many species. In addition, the roots of mangroves help hold soil particles together and create habitats for a variety of animals. Many mangrove forests develop near coral reefs, and their presence protects the reefs from silt and sediment that can smother coral animals. The loss of mangrove forests is currently a serious environmental problem in Thailand.

Conclusion

At one time, fish were only consumed by inhabitants of coastal regions, but today marine fisheries are international companies. As the public learns about the health benefits of eating fish, demand continues to grows. In some parts of the world, fish populations are being overexploited to meet consumer needs. Modern fishing technologies make it possible for fishermen to harvest almost any species from the sea.

As technology improves, so does fishing equipment. Until the mid-1990s, purse seine fishing efficiently captured tons of targeted fish, along with an almost equal volume of bycatch. To prevent the loss of so much sea life, purse seine nets have been outlawed. The same is true of drift nets, which are banned because they endanger the survival of marine turtles, birds, and mammals. Longlines and traps are traditional fishing techniques that produce less bycatch.

In many seas, like those off the coast of New England, several species have been completely fished out. The entire food chain of the region has been disrupted, and fish populations may never come back to their former size. For example, the

George's Bank cod population has been diminished by 77 percent since 1978. When these and other stocks reach such small numbers, there are not enough breeding adults left to replenish the population.

Mariculture, raising fish, shellfish, and seaweed under controlled conditions, is a technique that may supplement growing market demands without reducing supplies of marine organisms. Currently, oysters, shrimp, and salmon are a few of the species being cultivated. About one-third of all seafood consumed today is a product of mariculture.

Mariculture presents its own ecological problems. Nitrogen from feces and unused fish food enters coastal waterways and contributes to eutrophication. Maricultured carnivores, like shrimp and salmon, consume three times their weight in food made from wild-caught fish. Although mariculture may well have an important role in the future, the industry is still young and in the process of solving critical problems.

As populations of humans rise, sustainable sources of seafood will continue to be stretched. In many ways, mariculture is offering hope to coastal communities where natural fisheries are imperiled. Like other forms of agriculture, to be successful mariculture must offer a safe product with minimal environmental damage.

4

Human-Induced Ocean and Climate Changes

The oceans and the atmosphere are closely coupled systems, connecting with one another at the sea's surface, the interface between the two. Processes in the two global regions are interdependent, so both natural and human-induced changes in one system affect the other system. Activities of humans are stressing these two systems and interfering with several of their normal functions by changing the Earth's surface temperature, intensifying extreme weather conditions, damaging fragile coral reef ecosystems, increasing levels of dangerous radiation striking the Earth, and altering normal patterns of cloud cover.

The ocean plays quite a few roles in the Earth's climate. Just like the atmosphere, the ocean is able to redistribute heat around the globe. Because water has a greater capacity to store heat than either air or land, the ocean can store the Sun's radiant heat and release it later, often in a different location. In the middle of the day or during the summer months, when heat is abundant, water absorbs it. When heat supplies are reduced, as they are at night or in cold weather, water releases heat energy.

When water is heated by the Sun, not all the energy is stored; some is used in evaporation. Evaporation, the process in which a liquid changes to a gas, requires energy, so it cools the air and the ocean's surface. Evaporation leads to the formation of clouds and rain, and it adds additional water vapor to the layer of gases that warm the Earth. When water vapor condenses, changes from a gas to a liquid, heat is released. This heat is added to the system, so condensation warms air and water. Heating the air through condensation provides some of the thermal energy that is responsible for the movement of air currents.

In addition to storing and redistributing heat, the ocean plays roles in cycling life-supporting elements such as carbon, nitrogen, and sulfur. Carbon dioxide enters the ocean in two ways, by dissolving in the water and through uptake by phytoplankton, tiny, plantlike organisms that float near the ocean's surface. Populations of phytoplankton are extremely large, making these organisms responsible for more photosynthesis than anything else on Earth. As they photosynthesize, phytoplankton convert carbon dioxide gas into carbon-containing food molecules. Phytoplankton also integrate nitrogen and sulfur into their cells, elements essential to cell growth and development. When they die and decay, the organisms release these elements into the environment.

Global Warming

One of the most serious man-induced changes in the Earth's weather system is an increase in surface temperature, a phenomenon known as global warming. Over the past century, the average surface temperature of the Earth has increased by 1.1°F (0.6°C). Global warming is caused by a number of human activities in agriculture and industry.

The clearest culprit in global warming is burning fossil fuels in vehicles and energy-generating power plants. The gaseous products of fossil fuel combustion are causing a normally occurring layer of gases in the atmosphere, the greenhouse gases, to thicken. Greenhouse gases include water vapor, carbon dioxide, and methane, and are able to absorb heat and trap it near the surface of the Earth.

The greenhouse effect, detailed in Figure 4.1, is a process that has been in operation for millions of years. Without the greenhouse gases, the Earth's surface would average a chilly 0.4°F (−18°C) rather than the actual 59°F (15°C). As sunlight passes through the mixture of gases in the Earth's atmosphere, several things happen. More than one-quarter (26 percent) of the light hits the clouds and is reflected back into space. About 19 percent of the Sun's light is absorbed by gases like ozone and water vapor, as well as by particles in the air. The balance of sunlight, 55 percent, makes it to the Earth's surface, but 4 percent of this is reflected back to space. The 51 percent that actually remains on the Earth warms the ground, water, and air.

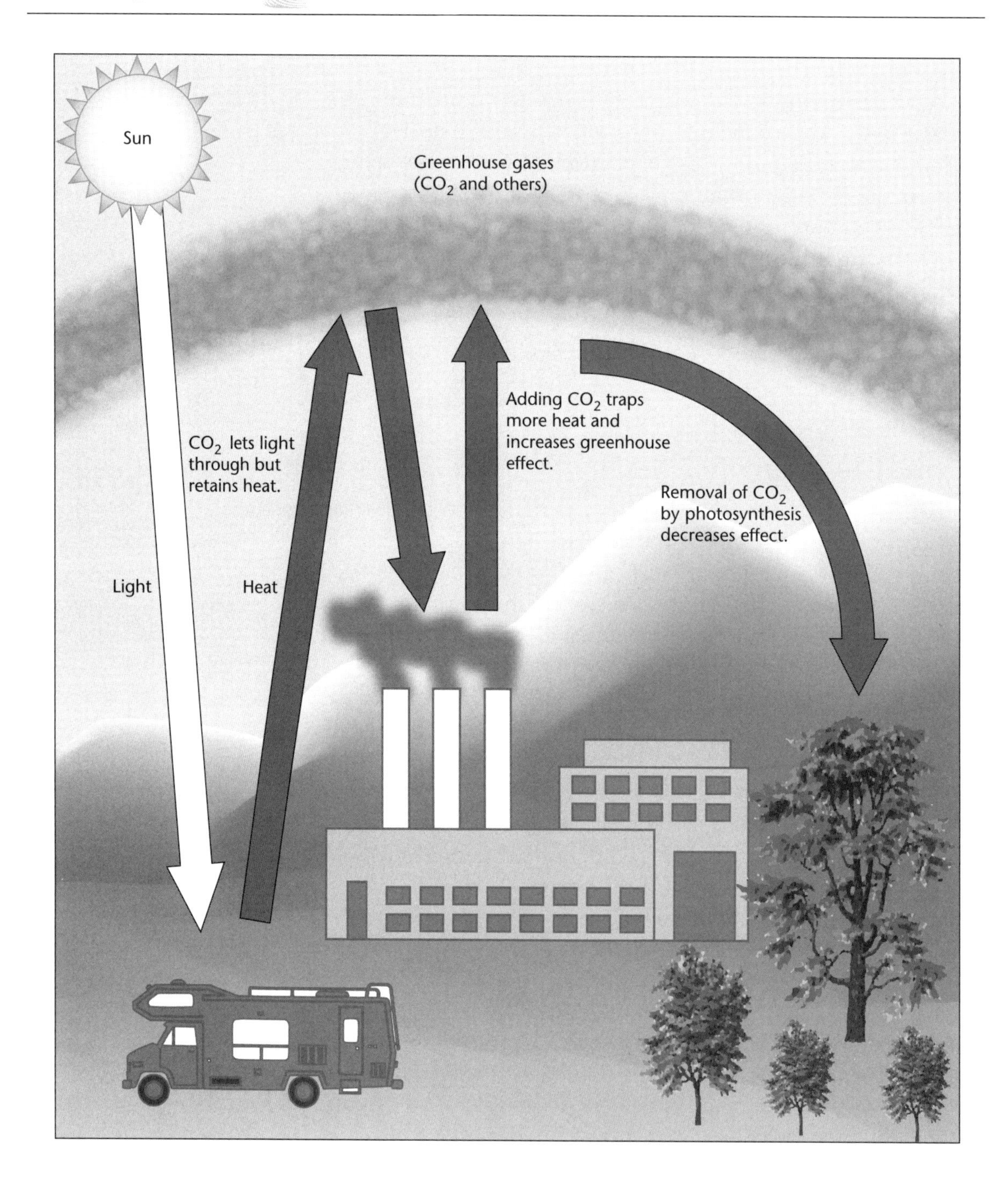

Fig. 4.1 Carbon dioxide is one of the greenhouse gases in the atmosphere that traps heat close to the surface of the Earth.

As the Earth warms, it begins to radiate heat energy away from the surface and in the direction of space. Very little of this energy actually reaches space because most of it is trapped by the greenhouse gases. The gases absorb the heat energy, become warmed by it, and then re-emit that heat toward the Earth. The Earth's surface is warmed once again, absorbing the re-emitted heat from the greenhouse gases, which it then radiates as more heat. The heat is continuously cycled back and forth from the surface to the greenhouse gases, keeping the Earth's energy systems warm.

The amount of energy absorbed and reflected back to the Earth by greenhouse gases is determined by the concentration of those gases in the atmosphere. Over most of the Earth's history, that concentration has remained stable, so the Earth's surface temperature has been stable. Since the beginning of the Industrial Revolution (about A.D. 1700), human activities have caused the concentration of greenhouses gases to grow steadily. Before A.D. 1700, levels of carbon dioxide in the air were about 280 parts per million (ppm), but today those levels have soared to 360 ppm, an increase of 30 percent.

Methane, another greenhouse gas, is also rising in concentration. Since 1750, methane levels have increased by 140 percent. Cultivated rice fields are a major source of methane gas. More than 90 percent of the world's rice is grown in Asia, with 3.2 percent in Latin America, 2.1 percent in Africa, and 2.5 percent in the rest of the world. Because rice fields are flooded with water, like natural wetlands, they harbor large populations of methane-producing bacteria that live in the waterlogged mud. Rice cultivation has climbed by a dramatic 50 percent since 1950. Other forms of cultivation, such as raising domestic grazing animals, have also contributed to increased levels of methane.

Scientists fear that these human-induced changes in surface temperature caused by the greenhouse effect could have negative consequences on climate and oceans, resulting in problems such as more frequent occurrences of extreme weather. To analyze and predict the possible outcomes of global warming, scientists create models of weather conditions and use them to make projections about future conditions. Computers interpret the data in the models and yield forecasts about just how much the global temperatures will change in response to increased concentrations of greenhouse gases. Most computer predictions suggest that a doubling of the concentration of greenhouse gases would raise global temperatures between 1.8° and 5.4°F (1° and 3°C). To date, global temperatures have already risen by 0.5° to 1.1°F (0.3° to 0.6°C).

Global warming has been occurring gradually over the past century, but some of its negative consequences are just now being realized. In the spring of 2004, the Scottish seabirds failed to breed. This devastating change in seabird reproductive behavior was directly linked to alterations in the birds' food web that were caused by global warming. Phytoplankton are sensitive to water temperature, preferring cool waters to warm ones. As seas have warmed, phytoplankton in some areas have thinned or disappeared altogether. Off the coast of Scotland, phytoplankton levels have been dropping over the past decade. A tiny fish, the sandeel, is the primary food of seabirds in the area. When sandeels first hatch from their eggs, they feed on phytoplankton. Without any phytoplankton to eat, baby sandeels died by the millions in the winter of 2003 and spring of 2004. As a result, seabirds had no food and were too weak and hungry to breed. This event is a tragic example of how global warming can collapse a food web from the bottom up.

No one knows for sure what all the costs of global warming might be, but scientists have some ideas. Sea levels are expected to rise, possibly as much as 3.3 feet (1 m) by 2100, due to melting glaciers. With less sea ice covering the polar oceans, the populations of phytoplankton may increase, causing changes in air and water temperatures as well as alterations in ocean circulation patterns. Increases in sea temperatures may also lead to widespread destruction of coral reefs, which are sensitive to changes in water temperature, and to changes in El Niño, a weather disturbance in the Pacific Ocean.

Adverse Consequences of El Niño

The activities of humans that cause changes in the oceans and the atmosphere can lead to modifications in typical patterns of weather and climate. One of the most studied normal weather phenomena is El Niño, an interruption in the usual ocean-atmosphere system in the tropical Pacific Ocean. El Niño is an extremely influential weather force that impacts climate all over the globe. For this reason scientists study past El Niños to determine what future weather and climate might be like.

According to geological evidence, El Niño events have been around for thousands of years, and their appearance every two to seven years is natural. During an El Niño event, warm water, with temperatures 32.9°F (0.5°C) above baseline levels, appear off the coast of Peru and Ecuador, usually around Christmas (leading to the name, El Niño, which means "child," in reference to the Christ child). Temperatures become elevated, and remain that way for three months or more, because the cooling trade winds that usually blow across the tropical Pacific Ocean die down. An El Niño event is detailed in the lower color photo on page C-5.

The increase in water temperature during El Niño augments the rate of evaporation at the sea's surface, causing a greater-than-normal amount of moisture and heat to rise from the ocean. When this happens, air pressure over the region fluctuates, a phenomenon known as the Southern Oscillation. The entire event, the El Niño and the associated Southern Oscillation that results from it, is referred to as the El Niño–Southern Oscillation (ENSO). ENSOs interfere with the usual flow of air currents and have far-reaching meteorological consequences.

Global warming has impacted the severity and frequency of ENSOs. To help predict ENSOs, thermometers and other data-gathering equipment is deployed on buoys, shown in the upper color insert on page C-6. Scientists have demonstrated that increases in the Earth's surface temperatures are responsible for ENSOs that produce unusually strong rainstorms and frequent flooding in some parts of the world, while spawning long, devastating droughts in other regions. The mechanisms of ENSO at the surface of the ocean are well known, but scientists are just beginning to understand some of their other consequences.

Because weather is closely tied to the ocean's surface, the effects of ENSOs in the deep oceans have always been believed to be minimal. Henry Ruhl and others at Scripps Institution of Oceanography, La Jolla, California, found evidence to the contrary. Ruhl discovered that even deepwater ecosystems are impacted by climatic changes. Observing life as far down as 1,451.4 feet (4,100 m) below the water's surface, over a 14-year period, Ruhl and associates found that severe ENSOs impact organisms on the deep seafloor. Between these weather disturbances, *Elpidia minutissima,* a sediment-colored sea cucumber, is one of the dominant forms of animal life at these depths. Sea cucumbers are tube-shaped relatives of sea stars that depend on organic matter that drifts down from upper layers as their source of food. After the powerful 1997–98 ENSO, levels of food increased and a different sea cucumber moved in, a white one called *Scotoplanes globosa,* while *Elpidia minutissima* disappeared. Such studies suggest that all regions of the sea may be more interconnected than once believed, and that scientists have a lot to learn about the extent of ENSOs influence.

Devastation to Coral Reefs

As some of the most productive ecosystems in the world, coral reefs provide homes to millions of unique organisms. The reefs, which serve as foundations for large, complex ecosystems, are constructed from the skeletons of millions of tiny coral animals. Each animal builds a calcium carbonate skeleton around its body for protection.

Corals are carnivorous animals that catch prey with tentacles armed with stinging cells. In the Tropics, however, most species of coral depend on a close relationship with one-celled green algae to support them nutritionally. Algae living within the coral tissues manufacture food for themselves through the process of photosynthesis. Some of their food leaks out of the algal cells and into the coral's tissues. Tropical coral reefs are always found in clear, shallow water, where the algae can receive good exposure to sunlight.

When water temperatures rise, the algae living within tissues of corals abandon their hosts. The loss of algae means that the corals are without their primary form of nutrition. If water temperatures return to normal within a few days, most corals can survive such a bleaching event. However, if temperatures remain high for weeks or months at a time, the coral animals die. Tropical oceans are influenced by heat produced by the greenhouse effect more so than other water bodies. While the rest of the Earth's surface has shown an average temperature increase of 1.1°F (0.6°C), tropical oceans have warmed 1.8°F (1°C).

Occasional coral bleaching is normal, and fishermen have noticed small areas of bleached coral for thousands of years. However, mass coral bleaching is a new event directly tied to changes in El Niño that have resulted from global warming. Some of the earliest cases of mass coral bleaching occurred in 1987 and 1990. These were followed by even worse bleaching events in 1998 and 2002. In the last two cases, bleaching followed El Niños, and damage was brutal. In 1998 water temperatures rose by 1.8°F (1°C), and reefs in 60 countries and island nations were damaged. One of the hardest hit areas, the Indian Ocean, reported more than 70 percent mortality of corals. In 2002 coral reefs in the South Pacific suffered the worst losses ever when surface water temperatures increased by 3.6°F (2°C). The Great Barrier Reef and other reef structures near the coasts of Australia experienced extreme bleaching, some reefs losing as much as 90 percent of their living coral.

The negative impacts of climatic changes on corals are augmented by other environmental stresses, all of which result from human activities. Global warming may be responsible for an increased number of tropical storms, which can also damage reefs by physically breaking them apart. In some regions, global warming results in more-than-usual levels of rainfall, a problem that augments the amount of sediment that washes into water around reefs. Sediment makes the water cloudy and reduces photosynthesis. In addition, the abnormally high levels of greenhouse gases in the air alter the acidity of marine waters. At the water's surface, carbon dioxide gas dissolves in seawater to produce carbonic acid. As levels of water acidity rise, the ability of corals to build calcium carbonate skeletons is impaired, so the higher the acidity of ocean water, the slower coral skeletons grow. Ocean water pollution is another serious problem for coral reefs. As the number of homes and businesses grow in regions bordering coral reefs, so do levels of pollution. The addition of fertilizers and sewage to waters near coral reefs increases the nutrient load, encouraging the growth of algae that can shade and smother the coral animals and their resident algae. All these problems put reefs under stress, making them more susceptible to bleaching and its devastating effects.

Limits to the Marine Carbon Cycle

The ocean plays key roles in the natural global carbon system, helping to regulate the amount of carbon dioxide in the atmosphere. Carbon dioxide in the air normally originates from a variety of sources: Living things release the gas as a byproduct of respiration, volcanic eruptions discharge large volumes of the gas, and the process of decomposition of organic matter also produces it.

Even though carbon dioxide is generated by all these natural sources, the biggest producers of carbon dioxide are human activities that involve burning wood or fossil fuels. Fuel combustion provides as much as 65 percent of the atmospheric load of carbon dioxide. Such high levels of this gas overwhelm the ocean's ability to regulate global carbon levels.

The ocean is part of the Earth's system of checks and balances that helps keep atmospheric levels of carbon dioxide in check. Three marine mechanisms are involved in carbon removal: uptake by phytoplankton and other green organisms, formation of animal shells, and incorporation into sediments. These three carbon-removing systems make the ocean the biggest reservoir, or sink, of carbon in the world.

Phytoplankton have a tremendous impact on the levels of carbon in the atmosphere and the ocean. Carbon dioxide in the air diffuses into the seawater at the surface where phytoplankton take it up and use it to make food. In this way, phytoplankton are constantly removing carbon dioxide from the air at the sea-air interface, preventing the gas from building up in the atmosphere. When the tiny organisms die and sink to the ocean floor, most decompose, releasing their carbon into the deepwaters as carbon dioxide once again. The decay of dead plants and animals maintains a very rich supply of carbon dioxide in deepwaters. The normal marine carbon cycle is illustrated in Figure 4.2.

Some types of sea life use carbon to build shells or skeletons. Clams, oysters, and mussels are a few of the organisms that take in carbonate and bicarbonate compounds, which contain carbon, and incorporate them into various types of shells. When these organisms die, they also sink to the seafloor, taking their shells with them and removing the carbon in those shells from global circulation. Corals use carbon in a similar way to construct their external skeletons. When corals die, their skeletons remain in place and provide homes for other types of organisms.

Fig. 4.2 Carbon is circulated around the Earth in a cycle. Carbon enters seawater from many sources, including the air, respiration by living things, erosion of carbon-containing rock, and combustion of fossil fuels. Carbon is removed by processes such as photosynthesis, the creation of limestone, and storage in plants and animals.

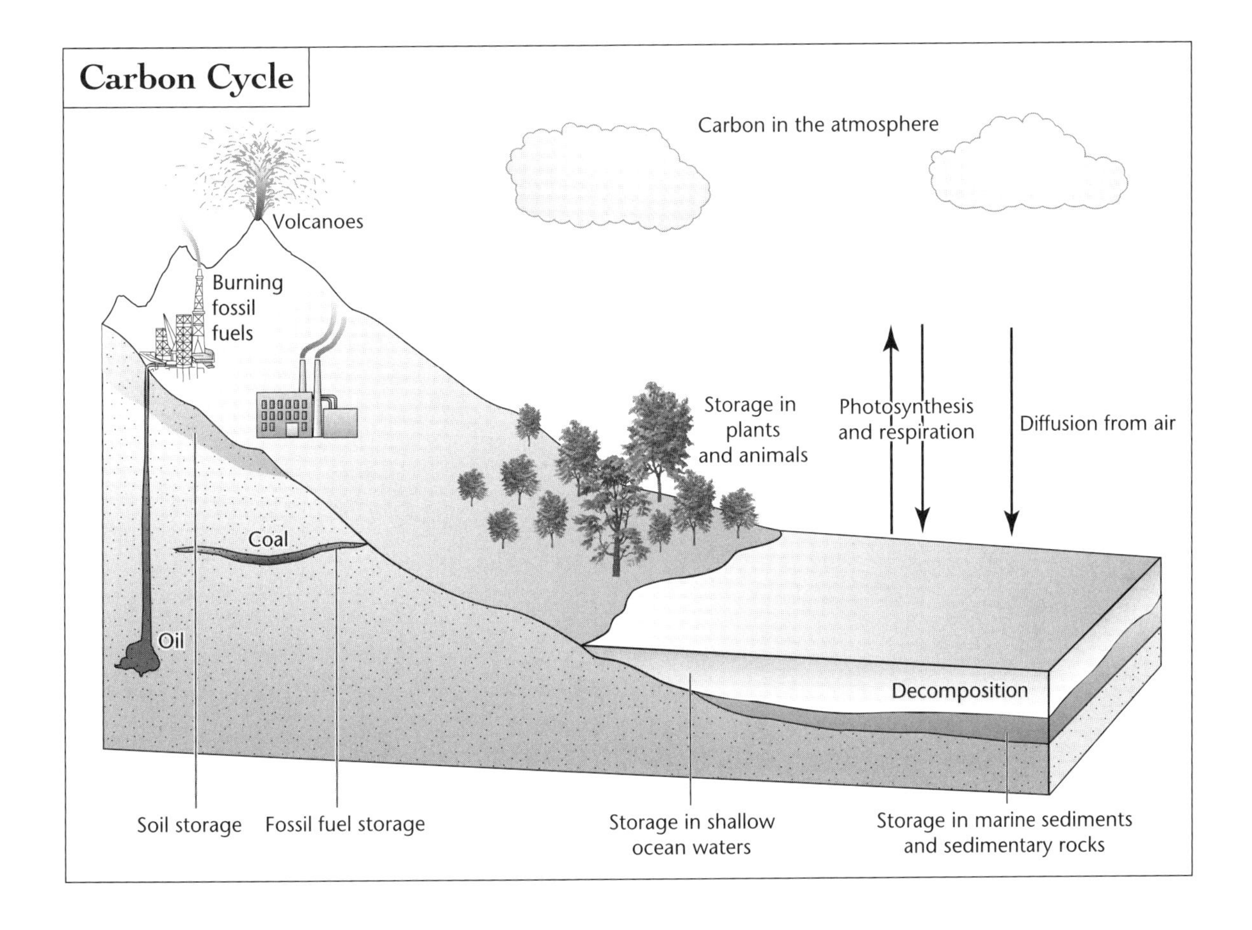

After death, most of the soft body parts of living things decompose. However, if the remains of organisms fall to the bottom of a shallow-water sea, they may become incorporated into sediments like limestone. Formation of limestone has a net effect of removing carbon dioxide from the atmosphere. The incorporation of carbon into limestone and other sediments is a very slow process, and it is cyclic. The weathering of these sediments releases carbon dioxide back into the atmosphere, replenishing the supplies lost to photosynthetic organisms.

Despite this natural system of checks and balances, the ocean cannot take in all of the excess carbon dioxide produced by humans by the combustion of fossil fuels. Some researchers are looking into ways to expand the sea's normal carbon dioxide storage capacity, and two approaches are under consideration. One is to enhance the productivity of phytoplankton in selected parts of the ocean since green organisms use carbon dioxide to create their food. Phytoplankton on the ocean's surface already absorb millions of tons of carbon dioxide. Experiments show that fertilizing the seas with supplements of iron could increase the rate of phytoplankton growth, and so increase the rate at which carbon dioxide is taken up. When the organisms die, they sink to the seafloor and take carbon with them.

The other idea is to store carbon dioxide in the deep ocean in the form of compounds called hydrates, solid or semisolid compounds that contain water molecules. To test the feasibility of this idea, researchers visited the deep seafloor and injected carbon dioxide into the water. Under the extreme pressure of the deep sea, the gas reacted with seawater and formed a hydrate, swelling into a ball of semisolid carbon dioxide. Deep seas might prove to be useful places to store carbon dioxide until it can be permanently disposed of in some other way.

Before either idea can be implemented, much research is needed. Increasing phytoplankton will have other consequences, so these must also be determined. The introduction of hydrates to the deep sea will also have ramifications for the deepwater environment. In both cases, long-term outcomes must be analyzed and the advantages weighed against disadvantages before any type of action can be taken.

The Ozone Hole

Although levels of carbon dioxide are critically important to the well-being of plankton, an entirely different man-induced atmospheric crisis, one known as the ozone hole, is also affecting their growth. Ozone is a gas that naturally occurs at two locations on the Earth, the surface and the upper atmosphere. Surface-level ozone, which represents 10 percent of the total Earth ozone, is a harmful pollutant that is produced by cars, industries, refineries, and other sources. More than 90 percent of the Earth's ozone is located in the upper regions of the atmosphere, where the gas forms a layer that protects living things by filtering out ultraviolet (UV) radiation from the Sun. The energy of UV radiation damages cells and impairs their function. In addition, UV radiation can cause cellular mutations, changes in the DNA that can be harmful. In humans, mutations caused by UV radiation are linked to cataracts and skin cancer.

Over the last half a century, the layer of ozone has been shrinking, damaged by man-made chemicals released into the atmosphere. Ozone-depleting chemicals (ODCs), a group of compounds that contain chlorine or bromine atoms, are used as refrigerants, solvents, insulating foams, pesticides, and fire extinguishers. All ODCs evaporate easily and, once airborne, travel slowly to the upper atmosphere, making the journey over a period of two to five years. When they arrive, UV radiation breaks the molecules apart, releasing the destructive chlorine and bromine atoms. Each chlorine atom that results from the breakdown of an ODC such as chlorofluorocarbon (CFC) sets off a cascade of chain reactions, resulting in the destruction of thousands of molecules of ozone. Bromine atoms are even worse, each one 40 times more destructive than a chlorine atom. Through international treaties, the production of ODCs in industrial nations has been phased out and substitute chemicals are being produced. Scientists believe that stopping the stream of ODCs entering the ozone will enable the layer to repair damage, perhaps returning to its original state by 2050.

The area hardest hit by ozone depletion is the portion of the atmosphere directly over Antarctica. Each spring the amount of ozone over the southernmost continent decreases by 50 percent, creating a region where the Sun's UV radiation can penetrate. Loss of ozone over the South Pole negatively impacts phytoplankton, reducing the rate of photosynthesis by 25 percent of previous levels. Antarctic phytoplankton populations are 10,000 to 100,000 times denser than those in tropical waters, so they are critically important to the world as carbon sinks and as the foundations of food chains. Damage to phytoplankton populations is harmful to the entire planet.

Exposure of phytoplankton to UV radiation reduces photosynthesis in several ways. Phytoplankton orient themselves in the water to maximize photosynthesis, using light, gravity, and other factors as guides. In experiments, researchers found that even moderately high doses of UV radiation damage the ability of phytoplankton to position themselves optimally in the water, thus reducing the amount of photosynthesis they can carry out. UV radiation also destroys some of the proteins that make up the photosynthetic equipment of cells. In addition, UV radiation interferes with photosynthesis by damaging the planktonic organisms that are capable of fixing nitrogen, a process in which they convert nitrogen from an atmospheric gas to compounds that living things can use. Since nitrogen is essential for photosynthesis, growth, and development, a lack of the element can interfere with the productivity of phytoplankton.

Reduction of photosynthesis in the Antarctic has far-reaching effects. Phytoplankton serve as the basis for polar food webs, and as such they are fed on by primary consumers such as shrimp and the larvae of fish. Large fish and other secondary consumers depend on the primary consumers for their food. In the same way, tertiary consumers, including fish, birds, and mammals, feed on the secondary consumers. A change in phytoplankton productivity directly affects innumerable food chains, including man's food from the ocean. A food chain that begins with phytoplankton and ends with humans is shown in Figure 4.3.

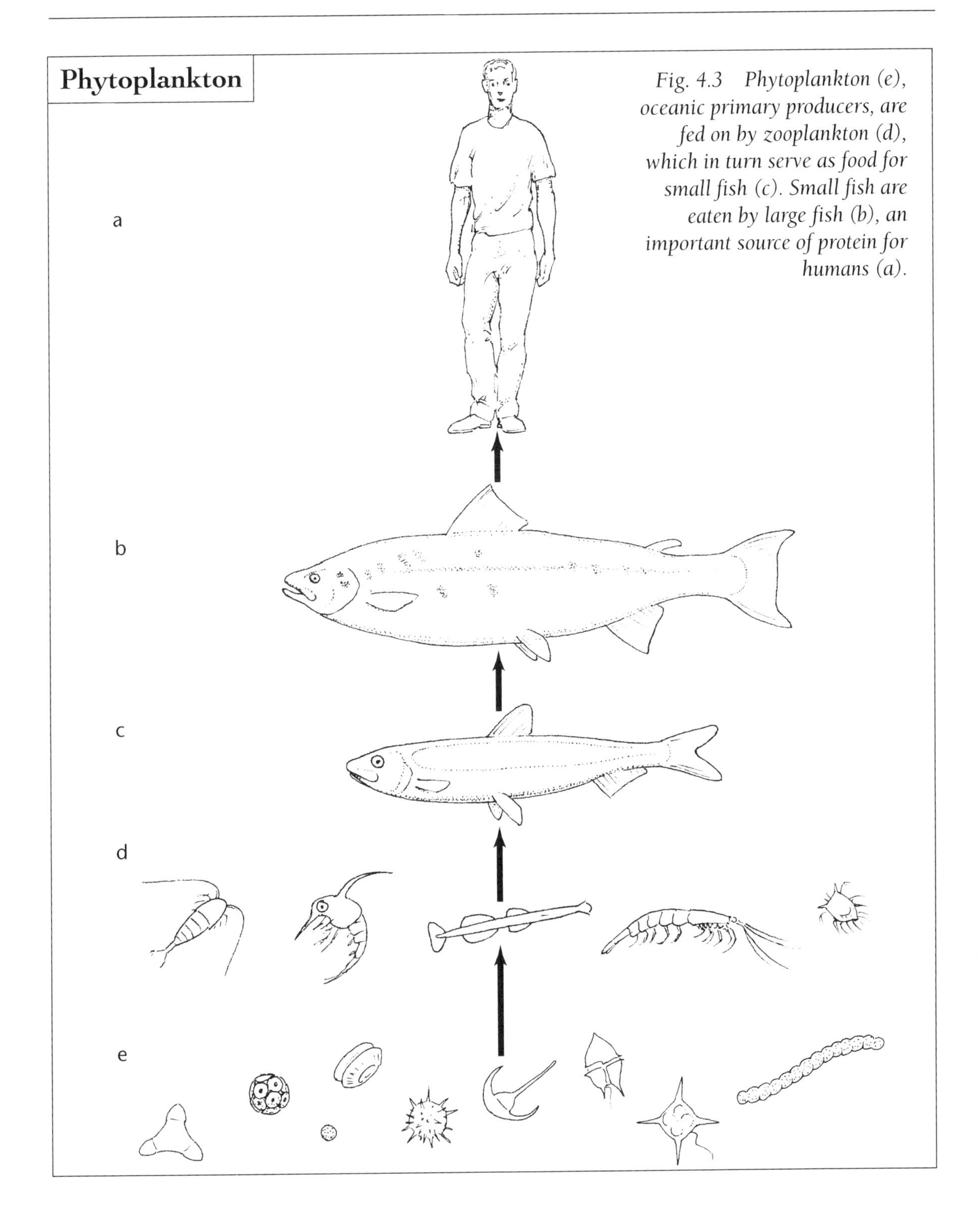

Fig. 4.3 Phytoplankton (e), oceanic primary producers, are fed on by zooplankton (d), which in turn serve as food for small fish (c). Small fish are eaten by large fish (b), an important source of protein for humans (a).

In addition, phytoplankton take up carbon dioxide from the atmosphere. The loss of just 5 percent of the world's phytoplankton would prevent the uptake of five gigatons of carbon dioxide, an amount equivalent to the carbon dioxide produced by worldwide combustion of fossil fuels in one year. For this reason, loss of phytoplankton would significantly worsen global warming and the consequences of it.

Consequences to the Sulfur Cycle

The functions of phytoplankton in the normal cycling of nutrients are complex and diverse. Along with their jobs as key absorbers of carbon, phytoplankton also play roles in the sulfur cycle. Sulfur, like carbon, influences weather, and the manner in which sulfur is cycled through the ocean-atmosphere system is linked to climate. Just as human activities are altering the ocean's role in the carbon cycle, they are also interfering with its functions in the sulfur cycle.

Marine algae and phytoplankton naturally produce dimethylsulfoniopropionate (DMSP), a compound that helps protect the organisms from the negative impacts of stressors like high salinity, strong doses of ultraviolet radiation, and freezing temperatures. The death and decomposition of marine algae and phytoplankton releases DMSP, which is quickly converted into the gas dimethylsulfide (DMS). When DMS enters the atmosphere at the sea-air interface, it is oxidized into compounds of sulfur that form tiny particles in the air. These particles act as seeds, or nuclei, for the condensation of water vapor, so they help form clouds. Because clouds reflect the Sun's energy back into space, they reduce the amount of sunlight hitting the Earth and have a net cooling effect. In this way, phytoplankton affect climate and are linked to cooling that could be critical to offsetting the impact of global warming.

The amount of DMS produced by phytoplankton is controlled by a feedback mechanism, one that stimulates the production of DMS when conditions are sunny and inhibits DMS release when conditions are cloudy. The natural cycle begins when phytoplankton in the ocean produce DMS, which leads to an increase in cloudiness. Cloudiness in turn reduces the amount of sunlight reaching the Earth, which lowers temperatures. Less sunlight also means that biological processes in phytoplankton slow down, reducing the amount of DMS produced. When DMS production rates drop, the rate of cloud formation also slows.

Because DMS production in phytoplankton is linked to the amount of sunlight, more of the chemical is given off in the summer than in the winter. In a similar way, DMS production

Food Chains and Photosynthesis

Living things must have energy to survive. In an ecosystem, the path that energy takes as it moves from one organism to another is called a food chain. The Sun is the major source of energy for most food chains. Organisms that can capture the Sun's energy are called producers, or autotrophs, because they are able to produce food molecules. Living things that cannot capture energy must eat food and are referred to as consumers, or heterotrophs. Heterotrophs that eat plants are herbivores, and those that eat animals are carnivores. Organisms that eat plants and animals are described as omnivores.

When living things die, another group of organisms in the food chain—the decomposers, or detritivores—uses the energy tied up in the lifeless bodies. Detritivores break down dead or decaying matter, returning the nutrients to the environment. Nutrients in ecosystems are constantly recycled through interlocking food chains called food webs. Energy, on the other hand, cannot be recycled. It is eventually lost to the system in the form of heat.

Autotrophs can capture the Sun's energy because they contain the green pigment chlorophyll. During photosynthesis, autotrophs use the Sun's energy to rearrange the carbon atoms from carbon dioxide gas to form glucose molecules. Glucose is the primary food or energy source for living things. The hydrogen and oxygen atoms needed to form glucose come from molecules of water. Producers give off the extra oxygen atoms that are generated during photosynthesis as oxygen gas.

Autotrophs usually make more glucose than they need, so they store some for later use. Heterotrophs consume this stored glucose to support their own life processes. In the long run, it is an ecosystem's productivity that determines the types and numbers of organisms that can live there.

also increases when UV radiation is high and when ozone levels are low. For this reason, loss of ozone around Antarctica due to the production of ozone-depleting chemicals means an increase of UV radiation on the phytoplankton, with a subsequent increase in DMS production and cloud formation. Scientists do not yet know all the consequences of this change in the normal cycle of sulfur but suspect they will influence the Earth's surface temperature.

Finding Solutions

To avoid future damage to the ocean-atmosphere link in climate and weather, scientists must first understand exactly how the systems work and where they are most vulnerable. Such understanding comes from observation, research, experimentation, and sharing information among researchers of different disciplines. Traditionally, most ocean research has been done from aboard ships and from monitoring stations along the shore. Nets, grabs, and dredges were used to catch, pick up, and scoop samples of marine life. One of the biggest advances in marine research came with the development on submersibles that could be used by scientists to study the underwater environment.

Submersibles, small underwater research vessels, and remotely controlled unmanned subs have enabled scientists to see parts of the ocean that have never been viewed by humans. In 1960 the submersible *Trieste* took a team of Swiss and American scientists on the deepest manned dive into the Marianna Trench. The submersible *Alvin* carried Americans back to the deep seafloor, and by 1977 scientists had discovered the unique communities of organisms that live around deepwater hydrothermal vents. *Alvin*, shown in the lower color insert on page C-6, is still in use, operated by the Woods Hole Oceanographic Institution in Massachusetts. Over the past 40 years of operation, the small sub has been modified to accommodate a pilot and two scientists. Scientists from the National Science Foundation, National Oceanic and Atmospheric Administration, and the U.S. Navy are petitioning for updated, modern vehicles that can carry more scientists, dive deeper, and stay under water longer.

A lot that is known about marine environments comes from analysis of data gathered over long periods of time. At this time, a global data-collecting system for studying oceans and atmosphere does not exist, although there are more than 40 independent, local systems and hundreds of smaller, specialized data-gathering structures scattered throughout the world. One such local system is the Southeast Atlantic Coast Ocean Observing System, SEACOOS. Like many other local systems, SEACOOS works closely with neighboring marine organizations to gather data from a variety of sources. All this information is analyzed to develop a picture of the weather and environmental conditions on the eastern coast of the United States. Many of the key monitoring stations for SEACOOS are located on structures on the inner continental shelf that were built by the navy to keep track of fighter jets for training purposes. Every six minutes, more than 15 instruments mounted on these structures measure factors such as air and water temperature, barometric pressure, and wind direction. At the same time, underwater cameras provide fishery biologists with pictures of fish, enabling them to study their patterns of migration.

Beginning in 2005 more than 50 nations, including the United States, will participate in a new project, the Global Earth Observation System of Systems (GEOSS). The goal of GEOSS is to gather and integrate information on coastal and marine environments around the world. By doing so, the system can help scientists understand natural oceanic events, as well as the impact of humans on oceans. The project, which is scheduled to last 10 years, will gather data from hundreds of sources, including satellites, ground-based weather stations, ocean platforms, moored and free-floating data-gathering buoys, and aircraft. Data can be beamed ashore in real time to provide scientists with up-to-the-minute information about weather conditions, air pollution, water temperature, ground tremors, and other statistics. Using data from GEOSS, scientists can improve weather forecasting, making it possible to predict storms with greater reliability. GEOSS will also help those scientists who are working to restore the health of coastal ecosystems and monitor ocean resources. Once in place, GEOSS can provide warnings of seismic events, such as the earthquake of December 26, 2004, off the west coast of northern Sumatra, Indonesia. Registering 9.0 on the Richter scale, the quake set off a devastating seismic wave, or tsunami, that claimed the lives of more than 200,000 people along the coastlines of the Indian Ocean.

Scientists at the National Oceanic and Atmospheric Administration (NOAA) have a system similar to the planned GEOSS in place around the Pacific Ocean. This Tsunami Warning System (TWS) is made up of 26 member states. From its center in Ewa Beach, Hawaii, scientists can monitor seismic activity in the Pacific Basin as well as along the coasts of Alaska and the western United States. The Pacific Basin system did not detect the Indian Ocean tsunami because there were no monitors in that region.

Conclusion

One of the most widely studied weather phenomena is El Niño, a disruption in the seasonal events in the Pacific Ocean that lead to periods of warmer-than-normal seawater. Although El Niño has occurred for thousands of years, its effects have worsened in the last century due to an increase in sea surface temperatures. In the last two decades, El Niño may have been responsible for extreme weather conditions such as storms and exceptionally heavy rains on one side of the globe, and drought and famine on the other.

The global warming crisis that has strengthened El Niño is a result of human activities that involve the combustion of fossil fuels. Burning puts carbon dioxide into the atmosphere, loading it with a greater volume of the gas than the ocean-atmosphere system is designed to handle. As a result, carbon dioxide thickens the layer of greenhouse gases that cover the Earth, causing them to retain more than the usual amount of heat. Besides augmenting the powers of El Niño, increasing surface temperatures have such far-reaching effects as disrupting food chains, raising sea levels, and damaging coral reefs.

Tropical coral reefs are extremely sensitive to changes in water temperature, so global warming can be devastating to them. When waters warm, the green unicellular algae that live in and among coral tissues and support them nutritionally leave their hosts and take up a free-living lifestyle. Loss of algae causes the corals to lose their primary source of food, a condition that can be fatal if it lasts for several weeks. Because the algae are responsible for providing corals with their characteristic bright colors, such events are referred to as bleachings.

Phytoplankton help reduce global warming by removing carbon from the atmosphere. Carbon that is incorporated into living things is cycled through the ocean-atmosphere system either as dissolved gas in the water of the seafloor, as the shells of animals like clams, or in sediments such as limestone. Scientists are examining some options for storing excess atmospheric carbon dioxide on the seafloor.

In Antarctica, decreased levels of ozone gas in the upper atmosphere may be responsible for a 25 percent drop in a phytoplankton production. Ozone protects the Earth's inhabitants from dangerous levels of UV radiation, which can damage photosynthetic machinery and cause cellular mutations. The production of ozone-depleting chemicals is responsible for the loss of atmospheric ozone. Changes in normal phytoplankton populations, whether through global warming or loss of ozone, have far-reaching climatic consequences.

To better understand how the ocean and climate are related, more than 50 nations are participating in a data-sharing project called GEOSS. Information gathered from this network will help predict weather and climate conditions. The reasons for predicting future weather conditions are varied and cover a wide range of needs. Improved weather prediction could help protect people and property in potentially dangerous zones, adjust agricultural activities to avoid devastating weather events, protect marine environments from weather-related damage, and minimize the outbreak of diseases related to weather changes.

5

Endangered Marine Life

Life on Earth shows immense diversity in form, so much so that only a fraction of the organisms living today are known to scientists. With environmental changes taking places at an ever-increasing pace, many species will never be known because they will become extinct before humans can discover them. Scientists have been aware of this problem for decades in the tropical rain forests but are just now recognizing the speed at which unknown marine life is disappearing.

Humans dominate the Earth and have expanded to inhabit most of the terrestrial environments, taking over or damaging the living space of other organisms. There is a direct correlation between the rising human population and rising rate of extinction. Since humans are terrestrial organisms, one might think their influence would end at the edges of continents, but this is not so. The pressure of people is felt far past their living quarters, spilling over into the enormous world of the sea.

The living space in the sea is vast, hundreds of times larger than the total living space on land. The three-dimensional quality of sea life provides habitats from top to bottom as well as from shore to shore. To humans, most of these habitats are unknown, and hidden within their depths are organisms that no one has ever seen.

People are more aware of the existence of threatened organisms on land than they are in the sea. Of the marine species, many people know that large mammals, like whales and seals, are in danger of extinction. In reality, the numbers of small, rarely noticed types of marine life, which make up the majority of species, are in as much danger as any. To bring public attention to all the organisms in danger of disappearing, many nations have established designations such as *vulnerable, threatened,* and *endangered,* signifying different levels of risk. Such labels bring national and international attention to the plight of these organisms, along with protection from hunting, fishing, and further loss of habitat.

Loss of Diversity

When a species becomes extinct, it is lost to the Earth. Loss of species leads to reduction of biological diversity, or biodiversity. The oceans have always been rich in biodiversity, containing more major groups of organisms than terrestrial environments. Of the 55 major groups, or phyla, of living things, more than 80 percent include species that live in the ocean, compared to 50 percent with species that live on the land. Some of these phyla contain thousands of different species.

The causes of loss of species diversity are many. Overfishing and bycatch, hunting, toxic chemicals, nutrient enrichment of waters, loss of habitat, alien species, and increased ultraviolet radiation due to loss of the ozone layer are some of the major causes. Scientists predict that in the future, changes in global climate will account for the majority of species loss. Since all Earth's inhabitants are connected and dependent on one another for survival, removal of one species sets off a chain reaction of events that impacts all others.

Loss of species diversity is just one way that a group of organisms can lose its variety. Diversity can also vanish on the genetic level and on the ecosystem level. Genetic diversity refers to the number of genetic building blocks that can be found among individuals in a species. The more genetic building blocks there are, the greater the level of variation in the genes of a group of organisms. Genes are made up of molecules of DNA, and they carry information that can be passed from one generation to the next. A group that has a lot of genetic diversity is better able to adapt to their ever-changing environment than one with little diversity. In this way, genetic variation gives population resilience in the face of a changing world. Populations that lose genetic variation become more fragile and subject to collapse. At a time when there is so much environmental change due to human activities, loss of genetic diversity in a population puts the entire group at risk because it reduces their ability to adapt to further changes in the environment.

Genetic diversity matters on many levels. A large, healthy population of individuals contains a lot of different genes, which can mix in endless new combinations to create variety among offspring. When a species dwindles down to just a small pool of organisms, these few individuals have only a limited amount of genetic information, and therefore only a few combinations are possible in successive generations. Small populations of species that are saved from extinction are never as healthy or adaptable as they would have been had they never faced extinction in the first place; they simply lack the genetic variability of the original group.

The genetic makeup of each group affects the entire ecosystem, the environment and all the other living inhabitants in that environment. A change that diminishes genetic makeup also generates ecosystem-level damage. At this time, scientists are not able to predict the long-term consequences of reduced genetic diversity on an ecosystem. Therefore, they do not know with certainty how destruction of marine habitats will affect the future of the oceans. Experience to date suggests it is dangerous to depend on populations with limited pools of genes to carry out all the functions needed for species survival, including passing on genes, coping with disease, and dealing with change.

A highly diverse ecosystem is home to a variety of species and supports a number of ecological processes. Examples of ecosystems in the ocean include sandy beaches, coral reefs, sea grass beds, and hydrothermal vents. All three types of diversity, species, genetic, and ecosystem, are important and interconnected, and must be preserved with each of these ecosystems.

Humans Cause Endangerment

The continued existence of some marine species is threatened by multiple factors, most of which are the direct result of human activities. Top among these is overexploitation, which includes overfishing and overhunting. Overfishing and the resulting large bycatches have put enormous pressures on fish populations. A new category of species depletion, commercial extinction, has been introduced to describe fish and shellfish whose populations are reduced so dramatically that fishermen cannot capture them in quantities that are economically feasible. Although not truly extinct, the populations of these animals are so small that they no longer play their traditional roles in ecosystems. Some of the marine organisms that have suffered from overexploitation include fish, shellfish, and marine mammals.

Nutrient-loaded waters and those carrying other kinds of pollutants cause stress to many organisms and depress the sizes of their populations. In these situations, species that are able to tolerate pollutants thrive and dominate the communities, changing the roles of all organisms in those ecosystems. These changes may lead to an even greater loss of species than the pollutants themselves.

Habitat destruction is a substantial problem for many species, especially in coastal regions such as estuaries and wetlands. The construction of homes and businesses, along with tourism and mariculture, destroys the integrity of the coastline and changes the natural ecosystems there. In many coastal regions, piers, docks, and marinas are erected, while in other places sea walls and jetties are built to redirect the natural distribution of sand. All these structures take valuable habitats out of the ecosystem.

The introduction of nonnative, or alien, species has had dire outcomes for some ecosystems. Nonnative organisms can be introduced into an ecosystem purposefully, as a new breed of fish that might be expected to boost local fishing, or accidentally, like a clam that clings to the hull of an international ship. Foreign organisms may cause no problems in local ecosystems, but sometimes they upset the ecological balance, causing the decline of native species.

Endangered Species Act

In 1962 the American biologist Rachel Carson (1907–64) published *The Silent Spring*, a book that brought to light the dangers of pesticides and other chemicals in the environment. Carson and other leaders in environmental education helped the public learn to appreciate the natural world. With increased awareness came the understanding that the ocean is an essential Earth ecosystem, not simply a resource, and interest in ocean organisms grew. In the United States, the first major legislation to protect living things was the Endangered Species Preservation Act of 1966. Although this legislation represented a step in the right direction, it only provided protection for native species.

In 1969 the Endangered Species Conservation Act was written to fill in some of the gaps in the Endangered Species Preservation Act. This second plan provided protection to species in danger of worldwide extinction. Significantly, the act also called for an international meeting to adopt conservation guides to protect species around the world. In 1972 the Marine Mammal Protection Act (MMPA) was developed by Congress to specifically safeguard and manage marine mammals and their products, such as hides and meat.

On an international level, the World Conservation Union, a group of scientists and nongovernmental and governmental organizations formed in 1948, put out a resolution in 1963 to develop a worldwide program of animal and plant protection. After 10 years of drafts and negotiations among all the member nation-states, a treaty was finally proposed. In 1973, 150 nation-states signed the Convention on International Trade in Endangered Species of Wild Fauna and Flora (CITES). The purpose of CITES is to regulate wildlife trade in plants and animals.

The strongest environmental law to date in the United States is the Endangered Species Act of 1973, which was written and ratified by the Congress to stop the extinction of species throughout their range. The act found that a number of species had already been rendered extinct due to practices in response to economic growth and that other species were so depleted in numbers that they were in danger of extinction. The act provided a means by which threatened species could be preserved.

The Endangered Species Act requires that species be judged "endangered" or "threatened" by several factors, including the changes in their habitats, overexploitation, disease, predation, and any other man-made factors that could threaten its existence. An "endangered" organism is one that is in danger of extinction throughout all, or most, of its range. A "threatened" species is one that is likely to become endangered in the near future.

Endangered Marine Plants and Invertebrates

Marine plants form the basis of oceanic food chains because they are capable of using the Sun's energy to make food. Despite their importance, several kinds of marine plants are facing serious threats because of human activities. For example, a shallow-water marine plant, Johnson's sea grass, is considered to be threatened throughout its range around southeastern Florida. Although most sea grasses are able to reproduce both sexually and asexually, this species is limited to asexual reproduction. In order for its rhizomes to spread, the grass needs a stable substrate on which it can grow. Some of the biggest human threats to the continued existence and recovery of Johnson's sea grass include damage by boat props, disturbance by boat anchors, dredging, storm action, siltation, and reduced water quality due to the influx of pollutants. Activities that unearth plants and destroy their root systems also sever the rhizomes and reduce their rates of reproduction.

All sea grasses rely on clear waters to provide plenty of sunlight for photosynthesis. Siltation caused by human disturbances increases the turbidity of water and reduces photosynthesis. Eutrophication, which stimulates the growth of algae in water, is also responsible for shading, and sometimes even smothering, beds of Johnson's sea grass. Algal blooms smother the grasses by reducing the oxygen content of water.

Invertebrates, animals that lack backbones, represent most of the animal life on Earth. Varying in size, shape, lifestyle, and habitat, invertebrates are found in all parts of the marine environment. One type of invertebrate, the tiny coral, is responsible for reef building in tropical waters. Corals are in trouble all over the world, suffering huge losses due to pollution, disease, coral bleaching, as well as damage by humans who drop boat anchors on them.

Around the Florida Keys and in the Caribbean, pillar corals, shown in the upper color insert on page C-7, grow up to 12 inches (30 cm) tall. Looking very much like the rounded knees of cypress trees, pillar coral are endangered and rare. Most corals feed at night, but this species extends its hairy-looking tentacles into the water during the day to catch debris and small animals. Overgrowth of algae due to the addition of nutrients to water (especially in the form of sewage affluence and fertilizer) and damage from boats and anchors put these animals on the endangered list.

Two of the primary reef-building corals, elkhorn and staghorn coral, are currently being evaluated as organisms that may need to be placed on the endangered species list. At one time both elkhorn and staghorn corals were widespread, often the most common corals seen in reefs. Since 1970 their populations have declined drastically, varying from 80 to 98 percent loss, depending on location. Areas that were once dense thickets of coral in the 1970s are now flattened and barren of coral.

Two types of abalones, or marine snails, are listed as endangered. Both the white abalone and the black abalone have been damaged by overfishing practices such as dredging and trawling. By many estimates, these organisms may be completely gone by 2010. Scientists are assembling a captive breeding stock in hopes of helping the populations recover.

Endangered Fish

Populations of fish are facing increasing pressures from overfishing, pollution, and loss of habitat. One endangered fish is the leafy sea dragon, an unusual relative of sea horses and a native of the coastal waters of southern Australia. Leafy sea dragons are covered in appendages that give them the appearance of leaves or blades of grass, so they live perfectly camouflaged in sea grass beds. In Australia, as in most of the world, the habitats of these small fish are suffering damage from an influx of water pollutants, primarily nutrients. In addition, leafy sea dragons are the objects of many unscrupulous collectors who

▲ *Much of the solid material in sewage settles out of suspension in large tanks.* (Courtesy of Damage Assessment Restoration Program, NOAA)

Dead clams wash up on a South Carolina beach after an oil spill. (Courtesy of Damage Assessment Restoration Program, NOAA)

▲ *A Hawaiian monk seal is entangled in rope.* (Courtesy of Fisheries Collection, NOAA)

▲ *Black-footed albatross eat garbage floating on the sea's surface.* (Courtesy of Fisheries Collection, NOAA)

▲ *On the deck of a shrimp trawler, a fisherman separates shrimp from the large bycatch.* (Courtesy of Fisheries Collection, NOAA)

◀ *A sea turtle drowned after it became entangled in a fishing net.* (Courtesy of Fisheries Collection, NOAA)

▲ *Floats (in the foreground) hold up a purse seine net, which is being used to encircle a school of menhaden.* (Courtesy of Fisheries Collection, NOAA)

▲ *Menhaden stored in the hold of the ship will be used to make pet food and fertilizer.* (Courtesy of Bob Williams, Fisheries Collection, NOAA)

▲ *The gillnet catch is hauled onto a boat.* (Courtesy of NOAA Restoration Center, Chris Doley)

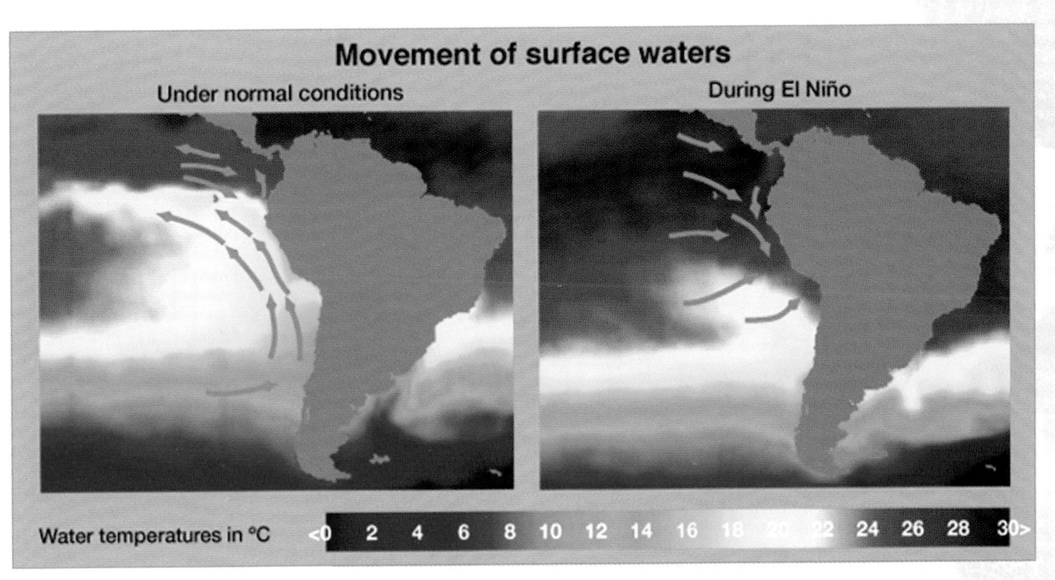

▲ *Under normal circumstances, winds blow away from the western coast of South America, pulling cool, nutrient-rich waters to the surface. In some years, winds are weak and surface temperatures are warmer than usual, a climatic condition known as El Niño.* (Courtesy of Fisheries Collection, NOAA)

▲ *To help them predict El Niño events, scientists monitor ocean temperatures at different depths from buoys arrayed with thermometers.* (Courtesy of NOAA Ship Collection)

◄ Alvin, *one of the earliest manned submersibles, has been taking scientists on exploratory missions into deep water for more than three decades.* (Courtesy of National Undersearch Research Program Collection, Woods Hole Oceanographic Inst., NOAA)

Populations of pillar coral are threatened by water pollution. (Courtesy of The Coral Kingdom Collection, Commander William Harrigan, ret., NOAA)

A turtle excluder device (TED) permits turtles to escape through an opening in trawl nets. (Courtesy of William B. Folsom, NMFS, NOAA)

▲ *During a coastal cleanup project, a pelican is rescued after it became entangled in a fishing line and was injured.* (Courtesy of NOAA Restoration Center, SE Region)

▲ *This manatee bears scars from a close encounter with the propellers of a boat motor.* (Courtesy of U.S. Fish and Wildlife Service)

sell them as ingredients in "Eastern" medicines, or as aquarium specimens. These delicate fish require exact conditions of temperature and salinity, and most die shortly after capture. Sea dragons are protected by Australian law because the demand for them has threatened the species with extinction.

In the United States, several types of anadromous fish are endangered, including sturgeons and salmon. Anadromous fish are not full-time saltwater residents; they are born in freshwater streams and then swim to saltwater environments as young fish and remain there for most of their lives. As adults, these fish swim back up the streams of their birth when it is time to breed.

Sturgeons, shown in Figure 5.1, are primitive fish with elongated bodies that are covered with five rows of bony plates or scutes. Most live a long time, reaching ages of 60 years or more. All sturgeons have cartilaginous skeletons, distinctive, tubelike mouths, and fleshy barbels, or sensory

Fig. 5.1 Sturgeons, such as the common sturgeon and the short-nosed sturgeon, are covered with bony plates. (Courtesy of Historic MNFS Collection, NOAA)

organs, on their snouts. These fish are bottom feeders that root around in sediment for food.

Several species of sturgeons are listed as endangered, including the shortnose sturgeon, pallid sturgeon, and white sturgeon. The shortnose sturgeon, which has been considered endangered since 1967, is not a target of the fishing industry. Instead, its populations have declined dramatically since the 1950s because these fish are often part of the bycatch of commercial fishermen. In addition, man-made changes in the habitats of shortnose sturgeons have reduced their spawning and nursery sites.

Populations of endangered sturgeons in the waters of the Florida panhandle may provide Florida some leverage in its ongoing water war with Georgia. Currently, Georgia has several dams along the Chattahoochee River that provide water to Atlanta and other cities. Florida contends that water in the Chattahoochee should flow unimpeded to the Gulf, assuring that sturgeon spawning sites and nurseries remain intact. The Endangered Species Act may tip the scale in the favor of Florida in settling this long-fought argument.

The numbers of salmon living in natural populations are extremely low, and their demise is due to several problems. Fishing pressure has reduced the stock of reproducing adults and decimated the genetic variability of salmon. Ozone depletion from the use of ozone-damaging chemicals is constantly damaging the standing stock of phytoplankton, which impacts their food supplies. Salmon require clear, fast-moving, highly oxygenated water in the streams when they return to breed. Pesticides poison their streams, and polluting nutrients fill those streams with algae, clouding them and sharply limiting the amount of suitable nesting sites.

At one time, some of the world's largest populations of salmon could be found in the Columbia and Snake Rivers of the northwestern United States. Now, only small groups of 12 different species, all threatened and endangered, live there. The decline in these particular salmon populations is largely due to the presence of dams in spawning rivers. Dams physically interfere with salmons' ability to return to the streams of their birth for spawning. In addition, power plants associated with dams generate warm water. During summer months, waters in the Snake River can exceed 68°F (20°C) and prove lethal to adult salmon.

Other widespread problems in the area include lowland agricultural practices that divert and pollute streams, as well as poor management of riparian regions, areas that border creeks and rivers. When streams are not protected by zones of natural vegetation, runoff from farms, industries, and homes flows into the stream waters and degrades their quality. Since 1991, 26 species of salmon have been listed as endangered.

Fish that spend their entire lives in the sea are also in trouble. Populations of several oceanic species, such as cod, haddock, and whiting, are dropping fast. Scientists from around the world are warning that in the North Sea, these species are close to collapse. In the Tropics, the Warsaw grouper is suffering a similar plight. A resident of deep, cold-water reefs, the grouper has been drastically overfished, and its populations are extremely low.

Several species of sharks are designated as vulnerable or endangered. Most threatened sharks are victims of bycatch rather than targets of fisheries, but a few species are being purposefully pursued. The increasing popularity of foods such as fish-and-chips, often sold under the name of "rock salmon," and shark-fin soup, an Asian delicacy, are hurting their populations. Like other fish that exist at the top of the food chain, sharks have always enjoyed predator-free environments. In the past most of these animals lived long lives, during which they experienced dozens of reproductive years. For this reason their reproductive strategies are slow, very much like those of mammals. Sharks reach sexual maturity late in life and produce only a few offspring. This type of reproductive strategy makes it very hard for damaged populations to recover. Some scientists predict that sharks will be the first species of fish to become extinct.

One of the most docile species is the gray nurse shark, which is now critically endangered along the coast of Australia and in other parts of the world. Although not known to attack humans, just a few decades ago these slow-moving fish eaters were mistakenly viewed as threats, and they were almost hunted to extinction. In the 1970s spear-hunting gray nurse sharks was a popular sport. Officials believe that only 300 to 500 grey nurse sharks are left in Australian waters. Populations in other parts of the world are not as well known.

The great white shark, portrayed as a vicious killer in films and novels, is declining rapidly, and in Australian waters it is listed as a vulnerable species. Great whites are part of the bycatch of longliners and net fishermen, who accidentally snare and kill between 100 and 440 each year. The black-market trade in shark products, such as jaws, teeth, and fins, is also significant. Shark fins, which are dried and sold as the chief ingredient in shark fin soup, bring more profit for the unscrupulous fisherman than the rest of the shark's body. For this reason, poachers often cut off the fins of a shark and throw the rest of the animal back in the ocean.

Basking sharks and whale sharks, the two largest species of fish in the world, are endangered and receive protection in U.S. waters as well as in those of many other countries. These two species are the only fish recognized as endangered by CITES. Unlike most other kinds of sharks, the whale and basking sharks are filter feeders that depend on plankton for food. Basking sharks can grow to 32.8 feet (10 m) long, and whale sharks as long as 65.6 feet (20 m). Both groups are targets of finning because poachers can sell their 6.6-foot (2 m)-long fins for as much as $15,000 each.

Smalltooth sawfish are relatives of sharks and rays. Named for their long, flat, sawlike snouts that are edged in teeth, smalltooth sawfish use these appendages to locate, stun, and kill prey such as fish and crustaceans. On the average, smalltooth sawfish reach about 18 feet (5.5 m) in length and can live about 30 years. At one time they ranged from the Gulf of Mexico to the coast of North Carolina, flourishing in shallow coastal waters and estuaries as well as freshwater lakes, ponds, rivers and streams. With populations reduced by about 99 percent, the fish are limited to the Florida Keys and Everglades National Park. Smalltooth sawfish are extremely vulnerable to entanglement in nets, longlines, and trawls, so they are frequently the victims of bycatch. In addition, the ecosystems where they live, nearshore environments, are some of the hardest hit by pollutants. Like other sharks, they have very slow growth and reproductive rates.

Endangered Reptiles

No other group of animals is more at risk of extinction than the sea turtles, large marine reptiles whose bodies are highly modified for life in the ocean. In the past overhunting severely depleted their populations. Today the few surviving turtles must contend with less direct, yet just as lethal, pressures from humans such as water pollution, fishing, and habitat destruction.

All species of sea turtles are either classified as endangered or threatened: the green sea turtle, hawksbill turtle, Kemp's ridley turtle, leatherback turtle, loggerhead turtle, and Olive ridley turtle. As a group, these animals face threats during all phases of their lives that are both natural and human-caused. The eggs are threatened by predators like raccoons and crabs that dig into nests to feed. Hatchlings scramble across wide expanses of sand, dodging seabirds on the sand and fish in the water. Only as adults are sea turtles free of predation, except for encounters with sharks. Scientists estimate that only one of as many as 10,000 hatchlings ever reaches maturity.

All these natural threats, which are serious obstacles to reaching maturity, pale in comparison to threats caused by humans. In some cultures, people slaughter adult turtles for meat, even though the acts are illegal in most countries. The shells are sought for making jewelry, especially the beautiful brown and gold-toned shells of hawksbill turtles. Commercial fishing kills thousands of turtles each year when the animals become tangled in fish nets and drown. At one time, shrimp nets were the cause of death to 55,000 sea turtles a year off the coasts of the southeastern United States alone. Today shrimp trawlers are required to put turtle excluder devices (TEDs) in their trawl nets. A TED, shown in the lower color insert on page C-7, is made of a grid of bars and nets that has an opening at either the top or bottom. The grid fits into the neck of a shrimp trawl net. Large animals like turtles and sharks are ejected through the opening.

Trash in the ocean, especially plastic, is deadly to turtles. Each year, thousands die when they mistake objects like plastic bags, balloons, and Styrofoam cups for jellyfish, their primary food. Plastic blocks their digestives systems, causing the reptiles to starve to death. In addition, changes to coastlines have had tremendous impacts on turtles, which need quiet, sandy beaches for nesting. Beaches are lined with homes, hotels, and businesses, and they are protected by seawalls and sandbags, all of which confuse and block the females at nesting time. Sand that is pumped onto beaches from other sites to augment beach size is often tightly packed and unsuitable for nests. Outdoor floodlights and bright streetlights may prevent females from climbing onto the beach, or disorient the hatchlings when they make their runs for the water. Water pollution is contributing to an increase in fibropapillomas, a disease that kills turtles. Other pollutants are toxic to marine algae, one of their important sources of food.

Endangered Birds

Like all other sea animals, birds are exposed to risks created by humans, such as pollution, overhunting, and loss of habitat. Because seabirds mature slowly, and pairs generally lay only one egg a year, their reproductive rates are very low. As a result, even after endangering activities stop, populations of the animals recover slowly. For this reason, several species of seabirds are endangered.

All the 21 species of albatross are facing problems, and six species are listed as endangered. Longline fishing creates trouble for albatrosses, causing the small populations to continue to wane. Always on the lookout for food, the birds spot the baited hooks just as longline fishermen throw them overboard. The albatross dive for the food on the hooks, get the hooks caught in their throats, and are pulled underwater by weighted lines, causing them to drown. In addition, albatross consume a lot of plastic trash floating in the ocean. They are especially attracted to red plastic, which the birds may mistake for shrimp. Plastic can clog their digestive tracts and cause starvation.

At one time there were millions of short-tail albatross in the North Pacific Ocean, but today populations are down to about 1,200 individuals. At the beginning of the 20th century, populations were reduced to extremely small numbers by overhunting of the birds in their primary breeding grounds in Japan. Building their nest on the ground made them vulnerable to hunters, and thousands of animals were killed for their feathers and other body parts. Today habitat destruction has greatly reduced their breeding areas, making it more difficult for the remaining birds to find suitable nesting areas.

Overhunting was also the death knell for piping plovers, a group of small seabirds that was driven to near extinction at the turn of the century when they were killed for meat. Protective measures saved several core populations and permitted their global populations to grow until the mid-1940s. After that time, the birds' numbers dropped again due to widespread destruction of their preferred habitats. Today there are only about 800 breeding pairs, with 200 building their nests in New York.

Newell's shearwater, a bird that was once abundant on the Hawaiian Islands, was in danger of extinction as early as the 1930s. Today these birds can only be found nesting in a small mountainous area. The human introduction of predators to the Hawaiian Islands, animals such as mongoose and black rats, made the ground-nesting birds vulnerable to attack. In addition, the shearwaters are attracted to light, which they use as a navigational tool. Hatchlings were often confused by urban lights, sometimes suffering night blindness, which causes them to fly into poles and buildings.

The brown pelican is a large coastal bird that dives for fish. Brown pelicans range from South America to North America, where they are more often seen on the southeastern coast and in the Gulf of Mexico. Populations were decimated during the 1950s and 1960s when DDT and other pesticides were widely sprayed to get rid of mosquitoes and crop insects. Even though DDT is banned, the birds are still threatened by other pesticides, loss of nesting sites, entanglement in fishing gear, and loss of habitat. In the upper color insert on page C-8, a volunteer helps rescue a brown pelican from such debris. Brown pelicans often make their homes in areas that humans choose for recreational sites, and the noise of motor boats may be upsetting their reproductive success.

Endangered Mammals

Since Neolithic times, humans have hunted marine mammals for their fur, meat, and blubber. The pursuit of seals, walruses, sea lions, and otters began with the earliest hunters and lasted well into the 20th century's era of commercial hunting organizations. Other mammals, such as manatees, dugongs, and dolphins, have also been the targets of hunting in cultures where these animals occur.

Cetaceans, or whales, are a group that includes large species such as the humpback whale as well as smaller animals like the bottlenose dolphin. Whales have always been hunted. Committed whalers have pursued their prey around the world, even when the populations of whales were so damaged that the species were nearing extinction.

In the 1900s whale hunters focused their attentions on animals in the Antarctic, taking factory ships, floating slaughterhouses where whale carcasses were processed, with the hunting fleets. At first only the largest animals were harvested, but as stocks dropped, the smaller, younger individuals were taken as well. Intense hunting caused populations of whales to drop dramatically until there was just a handful of adults left to reproduce. At this point, the whaling industry collapsed. The last known whaling ship wrecked off the coast of Maryland in 1924, and the final shore-based whaling operation closed in the 1930s.

When it began, the whaling industry was unregulated, so fishermen were free to take as much as they wanted. It was not until 1946 that the International Whaling Commission (IWC) was established. The IWC's original goal was to manage the harvest of whales for the benefit of whalers. As it became clear that populations of whales were crashing, the IWC developed into a conservation organization with its eye toward sustaining populations for the future.

In 1965 the IWC called for a stop to hunting blue whales, and nations that were members of the international commission complied. Nonmember countries continued to hunt the animals until 1971. In 1972, when the United States passed the Marine Mammals Protection Act (MMPA), whales fell under the act's protection. The primary government agency responsible for enforcing the MMPA is the National Marine Fisheries Service (NMFS).

In 1974 the IWC began protecting blue, gray, humpback, and right whales. By the time these species were declared to be in danger, their populations were on the verge of extinction. By 1986 the IWC called for a stop of all commercial whaling. Countries that abstained from the moratorium were Japan, Norway, and the Soviet Union, although the last finally stopped hunting whales in 1988. The Antarctic waters were set aside as a whale sanctuary by the IWC in 1994, but Japan refused to participate in this decision and continued to hunt whales there. Currently, Japan still hunts whales and uses the meat as pet and human food. Norway hunts Minke whales in the North Atlantic and kills 500 to 900 each year.

Today the National Marine Fisheries Service (NMFS) manages whales in waters of the United States. Figure 5.2 illustrates the estimated original global populations of whales and compares them to present population sizes. Some whale populations are making comebacks. Populations of gray whales have recovered, so they were removed from the endangered list in 1994. Right whales in the Southern Hemisphere and blue whales in the eastern North Pacific are doing better. On the other hand, right whales in the Northern Hemisphere are not faring well, and there are not many bowhead, blue, or fin whales in the Southern Ocean. Scientists fear that, for some species, the effects of whaling may not be completely reversible.

The dangers faced by whales today are different than they were 50 years ago, but just as devastating. Whales are now threatened by entanglement in fishing gear. The first large-scale bycatch of cetaceans involved oceanic dolphins that were caught by tuna fisheries in the 1960s. Public outcry against the deaths of thousands of animals caught in tuna nets, and the refusal of tuna canneries in the United States to handle dolphin-caught tuna, led to a change in fishing practices. However, cetaceans of all sizes still get caught in gill nets throughout the world.

Changes to environments caused by human activities are generally believed to adversely affect whales, but data proving

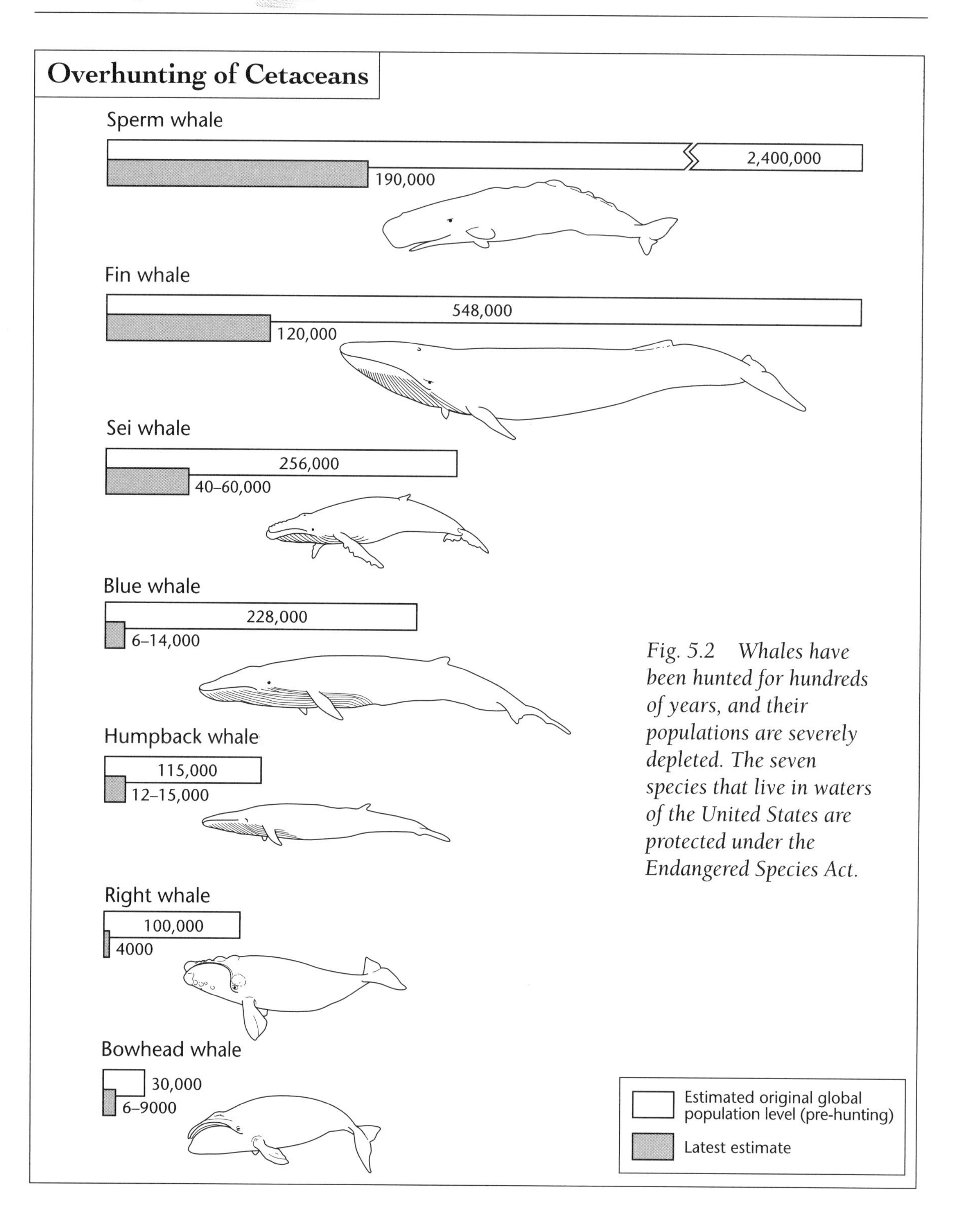

Fig. 5.2 Whales have been hunted for hundreds of years, and their populations are severely depleted. The seven species that live in waters of the United States are protected under the Endangered Species Act.

this assumption has been difficult to gather. Die-offs of bottlenose dolphins in the North Atlantic and in the Gulf of Mexico are not well understood but attributed to changes in water quality and environment. Polychlorinated biphenyls (PCBs), a group of chemicals no longer manufactured but that persist in the environment, are of special concern and believed to interfere with the hormones and immune systems of whales.

Whales use echolocation as a way of gathering information about their environment and are very sensitive to sounds. There is mounting evidence that sound in the ocean, including ship noises, military sonar systems, and seismic testing, may be disruptive to the animals. Scientists fear that these sounds may interfere with navigation, animal-to-animal communication, hunting, and other life-supporting activities among whales. To date, there are few studies, but anecdotal evidence suggests that much depends on the distance between the noise and the whale. Very strong, close underwater sounds have been shown to cause ruptures of tissues in the lungs and ears.

Under the MMPA, management and conservation of pinnipeds (seals) other than the walrus also falls to the NMFS. Pinnipeds have always been hunted by native people for their meat, which was used for food, their fur, a source of clothing and shelter, and their blubber, which provided oil. In the Arctic, seal populations were large and healthy until the late 1700s, when whalers and explorers from other parts of the world spotted the animals. In a short time more than 1.2 million animals were slaughtered for sale, and the populations were decimated. In the 19th and 20th centuries seals were hunted for fur, at first with lances, then later with guns. All species of seal fell to the brink of extinction. In many places populations are recovering, although Steller's sea lion numbers are small, and monk seals have not made a comeback.

Walruses, another pinniped; manatees and dugongs, a group known as sirenians; and sea otters, carnivorous marine mammals, are protected by another governmental agency, the U.S. Fish and Wildlife Service (FWS). In the 19th and 20th centuries walruses were hunted for fur and ivory (walrus tusk), and their fate was similar to that of other pinnipeds. Today there are about 250,000 walruses living around the Bering Sea, but populations are still considered threatened because reproductive rates are low.

Sirenians are a small group of plant-eating mammals, primarily found in the warm waters of the Tropics and subtropics. One member of the group, the Steller's sea cow, was first described in 1741, after which it was intensely hunted by whalers for its meat. By 1768 just 27 years after their discovery, the last known individual was killed. Relatives of the sea cow, the manatee and dugong, have fared better, but probably began with larger, more resilient populations. One of the biggest problems facing manatees is injury, as shown in the lower color insert on page C-8, caused by the propellers of boats. Because these slow-moving animals float just beneath the surface of the water, propellers have hurt and killed more manatees than any other factor in the waters around Florida.

Sea otters, like the one shown in Figure 5.3, have the dubious distinction of being the marine mammals with the most luxuriant fur coats, a feature that made them highly sought-after. Sea otters have been the targets of hunters since the 1780s. Even though these animals have been on the endangered species list since its inception, their populations are still

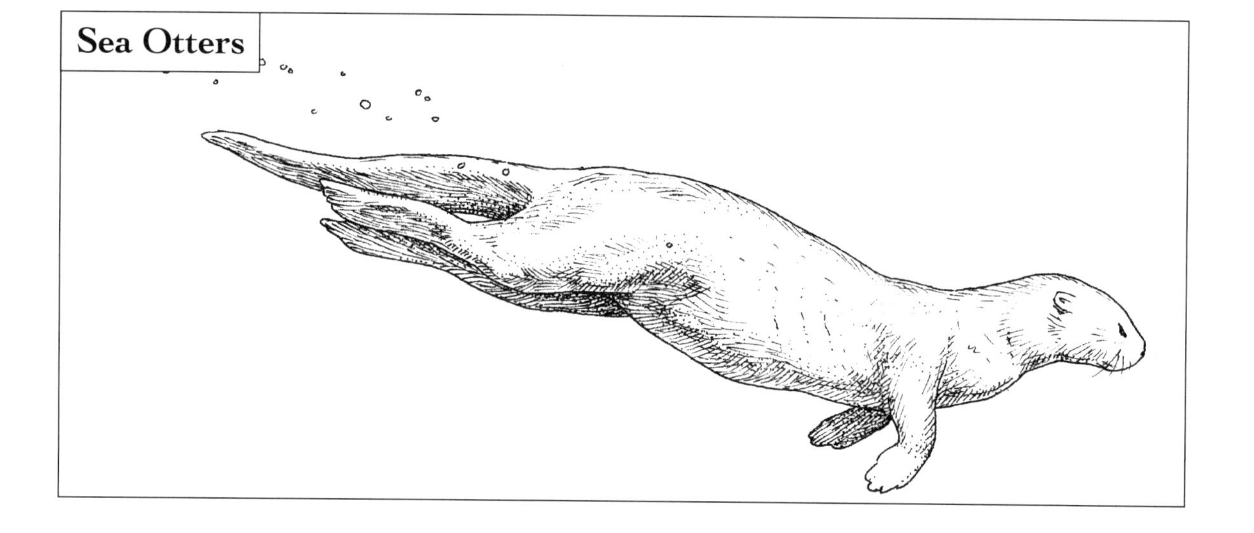

Fig. 5.3 At one time, sea otters were heavily exploited for their thick fur. Today recovering populations are distributed in coastal waters across the North Pacific, from Siberia to central California.

small in some places. Currently, sea otters range from Siberia to California. They are most often found in kelp beds, where sea urchins are the favorite food. One group, the California sea otters, is doing well under a federal recovery program.

Alien Species

Alien species, or nonindigenous nuisance species, are organisms that invade ecosystems outside their home range. Although most invaders cause no problems, some are capable of radically changing ecosystems. The infiltration of a new species to an area can be damaging for several reasons. The invader may be more successful than the original inhabitants, so it flourishes and uses up the resources that the native organisms depend on. In other cases, the invader may be a pathogen or parasite that decimates native populations.

An alien species can be introduced into a new ecosystem either intentionally or unintentionally. If the owner of a saltwater aquarium tires of the hobby and releases fish into a neighborhood estuary, that person has intentionally introduced a new species to the estuary. On the other hand, if a boat tied up in port in Asia unknowingly picks up organisms in its ballast water, the water taken on to help keep the ship stable, and carries them to a port in Florida, those organisms are unintentionally introduced into Florida waters.

On any day there are about 10,000 marine species hitching rides from one side of the ocean to another, most traveling in ballast water. Almost any kind of organism can become an invader, including microscopic plankton, fish, snails, mussels, and crabs.

Today there are about 75 different kinds of marine invaders in San Francisco Bay, while there are 35 or more in Washington State's Puget Sound and 28 to 32 species in the waters of New England. A few of the nonnative species living in San Francisco Bay include the European green crab, the New Zealand sea slug, the Chinese mitten crab, as well as several examples of clams, mussels, anemones, sponges, fish, and barnacles.

In the early 1800s European green crabs were introduced into eastern North America by ships. By 1989 the organisms had reached the West Coast, traveling in packing materials or attached to boats. The female European green crab produces 200,000 eggs a year, so populations of the species grow quickly under good conditions. The presence of European green crabs has hurt the New England soft-shell clam industry because the aliens eat mussels, clams, worms, algae, isopods, barnacles, and snails, taking food away from native crabs.

Conclusion

Biodiversity, the variety of living things in the environment, is an essential component of a healthy ecosystem. Diversity is important on the genetic level, the species level, and the ecosystem level. Loss of diversity at any one of these levels influences the condition of the other two.

In the ocean entire species of organisms have, and continue to, disappear. The reasons for some extinctions are very complex and involve natural causes, but the loss of others is simply due to overhunting. Steller's sea cows, for example, were killed for meat until all the animals were gone. In other cases, pollution, loss of habitat, and factors such as global warming have worked together to weaken species and make them more vulnerable to disease and predation.

The Convention on International Trade in Endangered Species of Wild Fauna and Flora (CITES) was established in 1973 to regulate wildlife trade in plants and animals. Shortly afterward, the U.S. Congress passed the Endangered Species Act to stop the extinction of species throughout their global range. Organisms close to extinction were ranked as "endangered." Once a species was officially placed on the Endangered Species Act, it was afforded protection from the factors contributing to its demise.

Marine organisms on the Endangered Species List include plants, invertebrates, fish, reptiles, birds, and mammals. Loss of species at the lower levels of the food chain, such as the Johnson sea grass, can also result in loss of higher trophic level organisms. In coral reefs, the staghorn and elkhorn coral, two threatened species, serve as the foundations for the development of complex communities and therefore serve as the architects of these colorful marine ecosystems.

Endangered marine mammals are some of the best-known animals in the world. Since the beginning of the Endangered Species Act, their plights have received international attention, and much effort has been focused on assisting in their recovery. Thanks to recovery programs and volunteer efforts, the gray whales, walrus, and many others are making comebacks.

6

The Ocean's Resources

As the size of the population increases and demands on the limited supplies of terrestrial natural resources dwindle, scientists turn their attention to the seas. The oceans are the world's largest reservoirs of natural resources. Food is one of the most important of these resources, but others include water, minerals, petroleum, building materials, chemicals, and energy.

Currently, only a fraction of the materials in use are derived from the ocean. Because submarine resources are more difficult to harvest than terrestrial ones, they are largely untapped. As the world begins to focus on these underwater riches, ecologists worry that an increase in the use of materials from the sea could damage its fragile ecosystems.

A Source of Salt and Water

The two largest components of the ocean are salt and water, so it makes sense that people should turn to the ocean for these materials. Salt, or sodium chloride (NaCl), can be removed from seawater, and the ocean presently supplies about 30 percent of the salt sold around the world. A few of the largest sea salt processing plants are located in France, Puerto Rico, California, Bahamas, Hawaii, and the Netherlands Antilles. The balance of the world's salt supply is mined from deposits on land that were formed when ancient seas evaporated.

To keep costs low, salt is processed from seawater with as little energy as possible. One frequently used, low-energy method of operation depends on evaporation. Seawater is guided into shallow ponds and allowed to evaporate. The salt left behind is cleaned and processed for the market. In cold parts of the world, where evaporation rates are low, water is channeled into shallow ponds and allowed to freeze. When water freezes, it excludes any minerals, like salt, that are dissolved in it. After chunks of ice are removed, the salty water left behind is heated to drive off moisture.

Water, possibly the most important compound to living things on the Earth, can also be derived from the ocean. Supplies of clean water are critical for every community of organisms. As the human population increases, so do the demands on streams, rivers, and underground reservoirs, the traditional sources of water. As a group, freshwater sources make up only 3 percent of the water supply; ninety-seven percent of the water on Earth is located in the oceans.

Before water from the ocean can be used in homes, business, and industries, the salt must be removed. The process of salt removal, desalination, is expensive because it requires a lot of energy. Currently, desalination plants only exist in regions that have no other freshwater options. There are more than 7,500 desalination plants in the world, with 60 percent located in arid Middle Eastern countries. Operations in the United States account for only 12 percent of the worldwide desalination. Texas and California currently run desalination plants, but these are designed to produce drinking water only. Desalination is an expensive process and cannot be used to provide water for agriculture and other nondrinking needs.

Salt can be removed from water in a variety of processes, but the two most common ones are distillation and reverse osmosis (RO). Distillation, the oldest desalting technology, uses heating, evaporation, and condensation, a series of events that mimic the natural water cycle. In a desalination plant, water is heated, usually with fossil fuels, to boiling. To increase evaporative rates and conserve fuel, some plants employ a technique that sprays salt water near a source of heat, causing flash evaporation. A multistage flash method water distillery in Saudi Arabia produces about 250 million gallons (946,500,000 L) of freshwater a day. There are currently about 2,000 desalination plants using a multistage flash technique, each producing freshwater at a cost of about $4 per 1,000 gallons (3,785 L).

In the process of reverse osmosis (RO), water is forced through a membrane that excludes salt. Before water can be processed in an RO plant, it must be pretreated with coagulants to solidify the salts. The membrane holds back these coagulated salts, allowing only pure water to pass through. In another type of RO system, a tube made of membrane is lowered into the sea. Water flows into the tube, but salt is excluded and left outside the membrane. The RO method keeps out bacteria as well as unwanted chemicals such as pesticides and antibiotics. In addition, RO is less expensive than distillation, costing only $2 per 1,000 gallons (3,785 L).

One major disadvantage of desalination is the production of a waste product called brine, a solution of highly concentrated salt water. Brine disposal is a problem for desalination plants. Brine cannot be returned to the ocean because it would affect the salinity of seawater and damage the environment, and it cannot be buried in a landfill since it would pollute groundwater. Currently, brine is stored in holding tanks, but better long-term solutions are needed.

Harvesting Medicine

Scientists are finding that the ocean is a rich source of unique chemicals, many of which have use as medicines. Biologists have long known that a number of marine plants and animals produce chemicals to protect themselves from predators. For example, many of the animal inhabitants of coral reefs, including sponges and flatworms, use chemical defenses. Most of these organisms are either slow moving or permanently attached to the substrates, so they cannot run from predators. For protection, their bodies manufacture toxic or foul tasting chemicals. In addition, some animals also produce a layer of slime that prevents bacteria from growing on their skin. Scientists are looking closely at these types of defensive chemicals as sources of new drugs and chemicals that can be used in research.

When scientists found bacteria living around geothermal vents and other blistering hot environments, they began experiments to find out how these organisms could survive

Zones in the Ocean

From the land, oceans often appear to be wide homogeneous expanses with wavy surfaces. Nothing could be further from the truth. Concealed beneath the oceans' waves are thousands of unique habitats and niches, each the result of one-of-a-kind combinations of light, temperature, water chemistry, and nutrients. Ocean habitats are found in both the water column and on the seafloor. For convenience, the waters and the ocean floors are divided into zones that are shown in Figure 6.1.

Deepwater regions of the ocean are referred to as the pelagic or oceanic zones, whereas areas above the shallow continental shelf are described as the neritic zones or nearshore waters. Below the water column is the seafloor, or the benthos. The region at the high-tide mark is the intertidal zone. Moving out to sea other zones are the sublittoral, bathyal, abyssal, and hadal.

The intertidal zone is the stretch of ocean between high and low tides. This area of shallow, tidal water is only found along the coasts. The sublittoral zone begins at the base of the intertidal zone and extends throughout continental shelves. Consequently, sublittoral substrates exist from depths of just a few inches to 656.2 feet (200 m). The sublittoral zone ends at the point where the continental shelf begins its sharp, downward descent.

The bathyal zone starts at the continental slope and includes the slope as well as the continental rise, a section of floor where water varies in depth from 656.2 feet (200 m) to 6,561.7 feet (2,000 m). Extending from the continental rise are the two deepest sections of the sea. Beyond the rise is the abyssal zone, whose depths extend from 6,561.7 to 19,685 feet (2,000 to 6,000 m). Below that is the hadal zone, which includes water that reaches depths of 36,089.2 feet (11,000 m).

such extreme conditions. These thermophiles, or heat lovers, live at temperatures that are lethal to other kinds of organisms. Scientists found that the thermophiles possess some unique enzymes. All living things produce enzymes, proteins that speed up chemical reactions, but in most creatures enzymes break down under high temperatures. Experiments on thermophiles show that their unique enzymes can remain intact and function in extreme heat.

This discovery led to the use of thermophile enzymes to solve some unique laboratory problems. For example, the

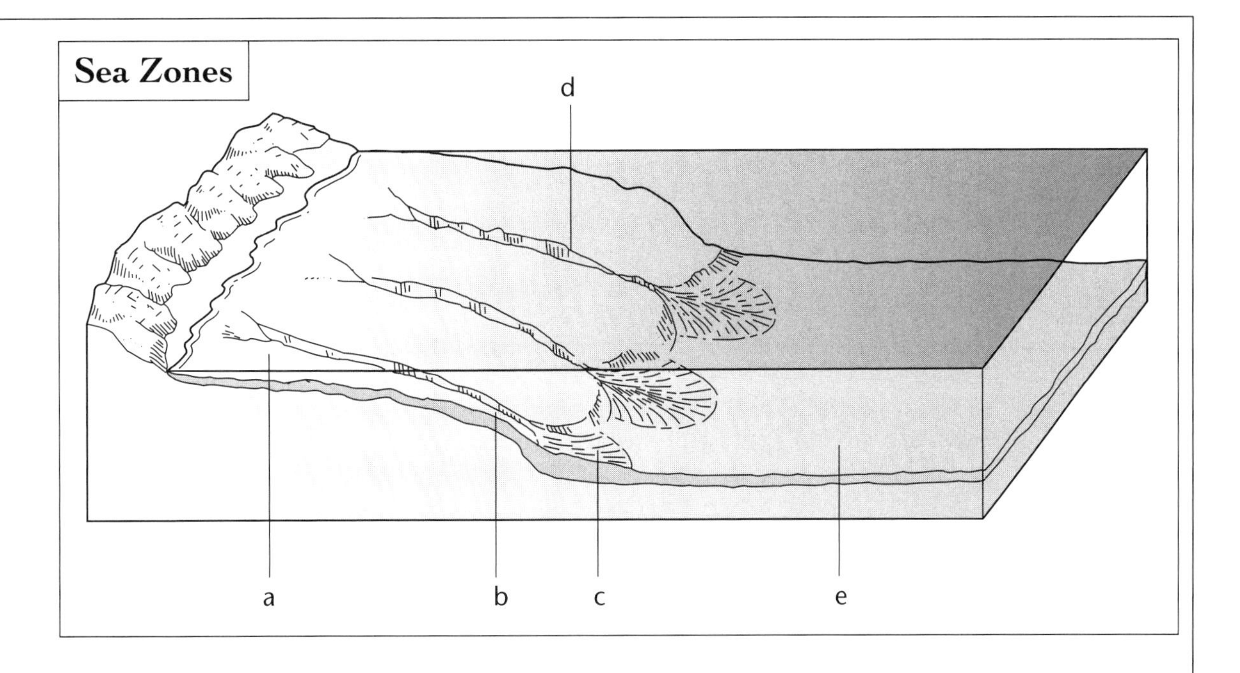

Fig. 6.1 The continental shelf (a) begins a downward slant at the continental slope (b). At the foot of the slope is the continental rise (c). Submarine canyons (d) can be found in some continental slopes. Extending seaward from the continental rise is the abyssal plain (e).

enzyme Pfu polymerase, one of the products of thermophilic bacteria, can quickly make thousands of copies of DNA under very hot conditions. When the Pfu enzyme was added to extremely small laboratory samples of DNA and incubated at high temperatures, the enzymes multiplied the DNA samples. This enzyme enabled scientists to create large quantities of DNA from originally small specimens. The technique of amplifying a sample of DNA has many applications, including use in forensic labs to help identify criminals from tiny bits of DNA evidence.

One of the best places for scientists to look for new sea chemicals is around the coral reefs. Reefs are densely populated ocean communities with a lot of biodiversity. Because competition for food and space is intense on coral reefs, organisms that live there are very specialized and produce a variety of unusual chemicals. The first medicine that was isolated from the sea came from a sea sponge that lives on Caribbean reefs. Found decades ago, the chemical was used to develop Cytosar-UR, an anticancer drug.

Chemicals are not the only materials that can be used in medicine; other ocean-derived materials are also useful. The hard exoskeletons of coral animals can be used as a substitute for bone in bone graphs. The exoskeleton of *Porites,* a species of coral, is similar in structure to bone and is commonly used in surgery. The calcium carbonate of the coral's exoskeleton provides a scaffold that can support cells as they attach and grow. For people who have lost an eye, coral exoskeleton can also be fashioned into eye-shaped spheres that fit into eye sockets. Because the chemical and physical structures of coral are similar to human physiology, the coral makes an excellent eye implant.

Marine Mining

The ocean is a rich source of minerals, but not all can be harvested in a way that is economically feasible. Some are too dilute in the water column or too widely dispersed on the seafloor to make their recovery worth the effort. In many cases, the minerals are simply too difficult to get to, like those in deepwater around hydrothermal vents. Despite these obstacles, several minerals are currently being mined for the oceans, and their production is a $500 million a year industry.

Most of the world's supply of magnesium and bromine come from oceans. Magnesium has been commercially extracted for about a century. In industry, magnesium is combined with other metals to form mixtures called alloys. Magnesium and iron alloys form strong, lightweight steel that is essential in the aerospace industry and in the manufacture of tools.

Bromine is not used as much now as it has been in the past. At one time, bromine was an important ingredient in the lead-based, antiknocking chemical additives for gasoline. Since the removal of lead from gasoline, this product is no longer needed, but bromine still plays rolls in the production of fumigants, flame retardants, dyes, and some medicines.

The most commonly mined materials from the ocean are those used in construction such as sand and gravel. As a group, construction materials represent 40 percent of marine mineral production. Sand and gravel are important components in the cement and concrete industries. In the United States the seabed is the primary source of most commercial-scale sand and gravel mines. Large deposits of these minerals are located off the northeast coast.

Sand and gravel can be dug from the seafloor with clamshell-type buckets, or pulled up by suction with sand pumps. Sand pumps are more popular than buckets but create more turbidity, or cloudiness, in the water. Japan leads the world in sand and gravel offshore mining, primarily because of the environmental restrictions placed on mining these materials onshore in that country. Offshore sand and gravel supplies are also critically important in the United Kingdom and in Hawaii, locations where terrestrial sources are lacking.

Silica sand and phosphate compounds are mined offshore for use in industry. Silica, or industrial sand, is the chief component in the manufacture of glass in Japan, northern New Zealand, and the Baltic. Argonite sand can be found in the shallow waters off the Bahamas, where it is mined by suction. The material is shipped to markets in the United States and Caribbean, for agricultural and industrial chemical processes.

Phosphorite is a mineral that contains phosphate nutrient required by plants. For this reason, phosphorite is an essential ingredient in fertilizers and a vital mineral resource for agriculture. Because phosphorite is abundant along most of the continental shelves, it is a potential source of fertilizer for Third World countries. Especially rich deposits of phosphorite are located in areas where nutrient-rich waters upwell, carrying minerals up from the depths. Some important regions of upwelling water are along the southeastern and southwestern coasts of the United States, the west coast of South America, and on the African coast in the Indian Ocean. Phosphorite is also used industrially in the production of soaps, detergent, and explosives.

In some regions of the seafloor, mineral-laden sediments accumulate on the continental shelves as placer deposits, sediments that contain a variety of minerals, including iron, tin, uranium, platinum, gold, and diamonds. For decades tin has been removed from placer deposits along the coast of Thailand. Tin is used in the manufacture of containers, solders, engine parts, and air and oil filters.

Gold exists in placer sediments near the coast of Alaska. To find the mineral, miners use 10-inch (25.40 cm) hoses that literally suck up the top layer of the seafloor. Shallow-water sediments, usually within one-quarter mile (0.40 km) off the shore, are pumped to the surface and dumped into sluice boxes, which separate the gold from other minerals. The unwanted materials are discharged back into the water. The University of Alaska at Fairbanks calculates that the sediments off the coast of Alaska hold more than 3 million ounces of gold.

Manganese is a constituent of polymetallic nodules, irregular spheres that can be found in regions of the seafloor that extend from the shallows to19,685 feet (6,000 m) in depth. The nodules also contain copper, cobalt, and nickel. Found scattered across 25 percent of the ocean floor, polymetallic nodules are most concentrated in the equatorial waters of the Pacific Ocean. By some estimates there may be as much as 16 million tons of these nodules on ocean floors. Although commercial miners have not yet developed a way to recover the nodules economically, they are still trying. In the United States, manganese is used to manufacture iron alloys and to make electrolytic manganese for use in dry-cell batteries. Alloys of manganese and steel are sensitive to changes in temperature, so important in making temperature-activated switches. Manganese also plays a role in the production of hardened steel, a material used to make support structures like I beams.

Diamonds, the only gemstone mined in the ocean, can be found in coastal deposits along South Africa. The diamonds in these sediments are derived from the rocks that produce the African diamond mines. To harvest them, miners dredge coastal sand and gravel at depths of 328 feet (100 m), then carefully sift through the sediments looking for gems.

Deep-sea geothermal vents are areas where superheated, mineral-laden water spews through the crust into the ocean. There are about 140 active, or recently active, geothermal vents on the seafloor. Hot water pouring from vents carries a load of metals and dissolved minerals. Many of these vents show little or no mineral deposits, while others are large and active, producing minerals in the water all around them. In the Trans-Atlantic Geotravers (TAG) site, an area in the mid-Atlantic ocean at the mid-oceanic ridge, there are a large number of geothermal vents with generous deposits of minerals. The regions around the vents contain millions of tons of sediments that are rich in copper, zinc, lead, and gold.

Offshore Oil and Natural Gas

Oil and gas make it possible for people all over the world to have electricity and transportation. Gigantic refineries convert the raw material, crude oil or petroleum, into products like gasoline, kerosene, and diesel fuel. Crude oil is also the basis of the petrochemical industry that manufactures plastics, fertilizers, and a host of other materials from oil.

Offshore production of oil and natural gas accounts for 90 percent of the mineral value of the ocean and generates hundreds of billions of dollars in revenue globally. Currently, about one-quarter of the supplies of these two resources are being mined from offshore wells. Geologists predict that the stores of oil and petroleum in the sea are large and may represent one-third of the Earth's total reserves. Significant stores of fuel lie off the coasts of southern California and Alaska, and in the Gulf of Mexico. All these deposits of oil and natural gas are believed to be on the continental shelves, with little in the deep regions of the sea.

Oil and gas come from layers of rocks called reservoirs that are usually associated with marine sediments. These two fossil fuels were formed from the remains of tiny, soft-bodied plants and animals that lived in the water and on the seafloor. When they died, some of these marine organisms accumulated in low-oxygen environments, where bottom scavengers were few. Eventually, their tissues were buried under layers of sediments. For eons sand and silt rained down on the sediments, adding to the weight of material covering these organisms. As time passed, the pressure and heat of the overlying materials increased, slow-cooking the buried bodies. The intense heat and pressure caused chemical changes that converted the tissues into simple hydrocarbons, compounds made of hydrogen and carbon. Over millions of years the burial grounds became oil-saturated rocks.

All the organic matter trapped in the sediments may not have turned into oil. Materials trapped for longer periods of time, and in hotter conditions, were usually converted into natural gas. That is why geologists search for natural gas in deeper, older layers of the Earth's crust, where temperatures are higher.

Oil is less dense than other sediments, so it rises above them, migrating up through the layers as far as it can travel. Eventually, the thick fluid hits a cap, a layer of sediment made of impenetrable material like clay that keeps it from rising any higher. Oil can remain trapped below a cap for millions of years. The deposits of oil may be as thick as tar, or as thin as water, and the color can vary from black to clear.

Drilling for oil in the ocean is more expensive than drilling on land. Even so, there are wells located on continental shelves around the world. In the Gulf of Mexico and off the coast of California, about 4,000 drilling platforms service thousands of underwater wells.

For an offshore well to be economically feasible, it must be a big producer, generating at least three or four times as much oil as a well on the continent. To recover offshore oil in relatively shallow waters, those less than 330 feet (100 m) deep, huge platforms are erected on top of long, thin-legged rigs. The platforms are often large enough to provide housing for the drilling crew and a base of operations for the equipment.

In water that is too deep to build a rig, floating platforms are used. These are actually self-propelled, bargelike structures tied to the seafloor with giant cables. After a deep-water well is complete, the platform can be lowered to the seafloor and sealed over the well to protect it. Oil rigs of this type have been used to drill wells in waters as deep as 7,500 feet (2,200 m).

Alternative Energy Sources

Oil and natural gas are convenient and relatively easy-to-use sources of power, but they have some serious disadvantages. Both are considered to be nonrenewable resources since they exist in finite supplies. It is possible that, one day in the future, mankind will run out of oil and natural gas. The combustion of these fossil fuels has negative impacts on the environment, causing problems like acid rain and the greenhouse effect. As a result, scientists are actively searching for cleaner sources of energy. The ocean offers four environmentally friendly possibilities: tidal power, wave power, thermal conversion, and wind power. All four are based on the same principle: Energy is used to turn the blades of turbines, and the turbines are attached to electrical generators.

Tidal power takes advantage of the gravitational pull of the Moon, using the differences in water levels at high and low tides. The largest tidal power plant in the world was built in 1966 in Saint-Malo, France. This plant includes a damlike structure called a barrage that crosses the mouth of an estuary. The barrage operates very much like a hydroelectric dam. When the tide goes in and out, water flows through the barrage and turns turbines. The Saint-Malo plant produces 240 megawatts of energy, enough to power about 240,000 homes.

Barrage-style tidal power plants are only effective in places where the difference in the heights of high and low tide is at least 16 feet (4.9 m). In the United States the areas where a barrage-style tidal power plant are feasible are along the coasts of Alaska and Maine. To offer tidal power in regions where high and low tides cover smaller distances, engineers have developed a different kind of generator.

A plant made up of six small turbines has recently begun operation in New York City's East River. Although each unit can generate only about 200 to 300 kilowatts of energy, enough to power a small neighborhood, this endeavor is the first power-producing tidal turbine farm in the world. Windmill-shaped turbines are installed in the river about 29.5 feet (nine meters) below the surface of the water. As the tide flows in and out of the river, the moving water turns the blades of the turbines. The heads of the turbines are designed to pivot to face the current, no matter what its direction of flow. By the time the project is complete, developers will have 300 turbines installed in the river.

Waves are one of the ocean's most noticeable surface features. Although it appears that water travels across the ocean's surface in waves, the only thing that travels in a wave is energy. Water simply moves up and down. The original energy that starts waves comes from several sources, but the most common one is wind. Others include landslides, volcanic eruptions, and movement along faults on the ocean floor.

The enormous amount of energy in ocean waves can be converted into mechanical energy and used to rotate the blades of turbines. Several European countries, especially the United Kingdom, Germany, and Denmark, are leading the field in wave energy and currently have dozens of offshore projects. In the United States a wave energy plant is being considered off the coast of Washington State.

In a wave plant, there are two basic elements: a wave energy collector and a generator that converts the wave energy into electricity. The wave energy collector is a sloping, boxlike container that is built into the shoreline. As a wave enters the box, it compresses the air in the top of the chamber, then forces it through an opening called a "blowhole" that is directed toward the blades of a turbine. As water moves back out of the chamber, air is sucked back in through the blowhole, pulling air over the turbine blades again. The turbine is designed to turn in one direction, no matter what the direction of the airflow.

Tides and wave energy devices are based on the use of the sea's movements or mechanical energy. Another source of energy, the ocean thermal energy conversion (OTEC), takes advantage of the difference in the temperatures of warm, upper-layer waters and cold, deep-region waters. OTEC works in tropical and subtropical regions, where the surface waters receive, and store, a lot of heat energy from the Sun.

Each OTEC plant has a large pipe driven into the deep part of the ocean, where water temperatures are very low. This intake pipe draws cold water off the bottom and moves it toward the surface. Depending on the design, there are two ways that the cold water can be used to create power: the closed-cycle technique and the open-cycle method.

In the closed-cycle system, thermal energy in the surface layer of water is used to heat a fluid. Heating causes the fluid to vaporize. The fluid is one that boils at a relatively low temperature, such as ammonia, whose boiling point is –28°F (–33.9°C). As liquid ammonia changes into a vapor, it expands and pushes against the blades of a turbine. Next the vaporized ammonia is cooled using cold seawater. As it cools, the ammonia changes back into a liquid. Immediately, the ammonia is heated again with warm surface water and the cycle repeats.

In the open-cycle system, the only fluid used is seawater. Warm water from the surface of the ocean enters a vacuum, which causes it to turn into a vapor. As in the closed-cycle system, the expanding vapor turns the turbine blades. The vapor is then exposed to cold water and condenses. In this case the condensate, the liquid that forms from the vapor, is pure water and can be used for drinking, or it can be returned to the ocean.

Of all the methods to generate energy one of the most promising uses offshore winds. According to the Department of Energy, wind power is the fastest-growing energy resource in the world. Wind projects established in several parts of Europe have performed satisfactorily. The constant, strong winds that are characteristic of offshore locations make them ideal sites for wind-powered energy plants.

In wind-powered plants, tall towers support turbines fitted with windmill-like paddles. Although an offshore wind energy plant does not exist in the United States at this time, the pros and cons are under review for the construction of a

Tides

Tides result from a combination of three forces: the gravitational force of the Sun, the gravitational force of the Moon, and the motion of the Earth. Gravity is the force of attraction, or pull, between two bodies. Everything that has mass exerts gravity. The Earth and Moon exert gravitational pulls on each other. Because the Earth has more mass than the Moon, its gravity keeps the Moon in orbit. The Moon does not fall into the Earth because of the inertia, the tendency of a moving object to keep moving, that is created by their stable orbits.

The inward force of gravity and the outward force of inertia affect the entire surface of the Earth, but not to the same degree. Owing to Earth's rounded shape, the equator is closer to the Moon than Earth's poles are. The pull of the Moon's gravity is consequently stronger around the equator. On the side of the Earth facing the Moon at any given time, the Moon's gravity pulls the Earth toward it. The solid Earth is unable to respond dramatically to that pull, but the liquid part of Earth can. As a result, the ocean bulges out toward the Moon on the side of Earth that is facing it. On the side that is farthest from the Moon, inertia flings water away from the Moon. The Moon's pull on one side of Earth and the force of inertia on the opposite side create two bulges—high tides—in the ocean.

The bulges do not rotate around the Earth as it turns on its axis. Instead, they remain aligned with the Moon as the Earth rotates under them. Different parts of the Earth move into and out of these bulges as it goes through one rotation, or one day.

Even though the Sun is much farther from Earth than the Moon is, the Sun also has an effect on tides. The Sun's influence is only about half that of the Moon's. A small solar bulge on Earth follows the Sun throughout the day, and the side of the Earth opposite the Sun experiences a small inertial bulge.

The Moon revolves around the Earth in a 28-day cycle. As it does so, the positions of the Moon, Earth, and Sun relative to one another change. The three bodies are perfectly aligned during two phases: new moon and full moon, as shown in Figure 6.2. At these times, the Sun and Moon forces are acting on the same area of Earth at the same time, causing high tide to be at its highest and low tide to be at its lowest. These extremes are known as spring tides and occur every two weeks.

During first- and third-quarter conditions, when only one-half of the Moon is visible in the night sky, the Sun and Moon are at right angles to the Earth. In these positions, their gravitational pulls are working against each other, and the two bodies cancel each other's effects to some degree, causing high tides to be at their lowest, and low tides to be at their highest. These neap tides also occur every two weeks.

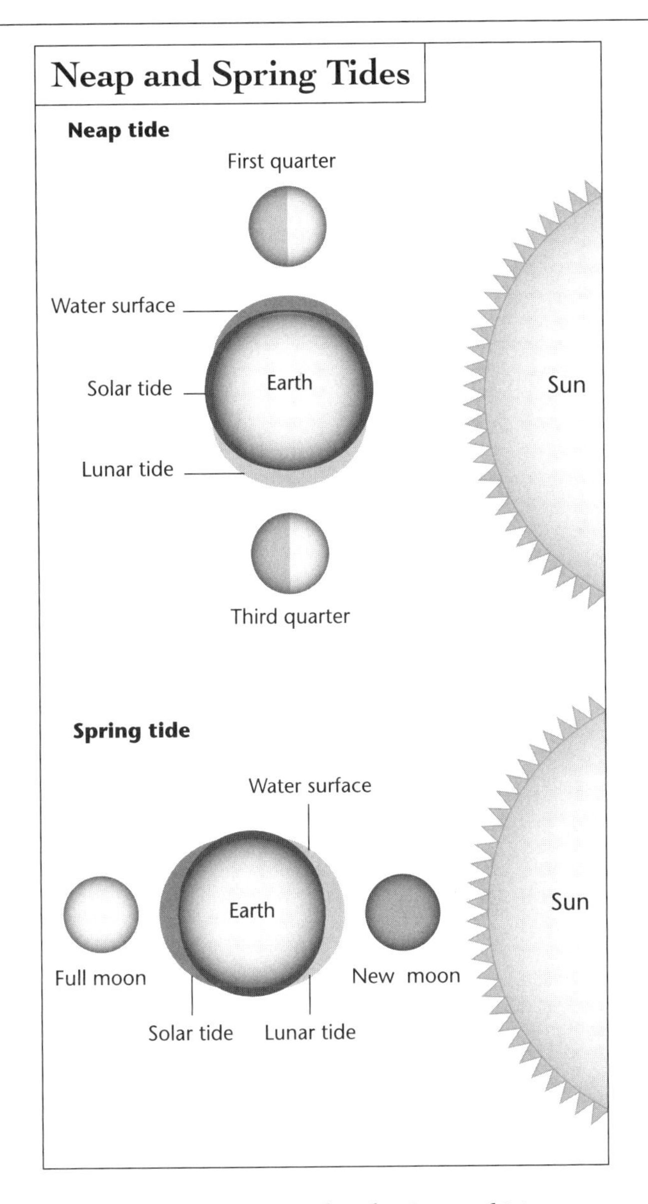

Fig. 6.2 Every two weeks, the Sun and Moon are aligned with Earth so that the gravitational forces of both heavenly bodies create very high tides called spring tides. When the Moon and Sun are at right angles to Earth, lower, or neap, tides result.

facility off the coast of Cape Cod, Massachusetts. Developers propose 170 wind turbines rising 420 feet (128 m) above the water. Such a plant will be capable of producing about 160 megawatts of energy a year.

Conclusion

Water and salt, the two most common components of seawater, can be recovered from the ocean. In coastal countries where rainfall is infrequent, desalination plants are important sources of water. Seawater can be desalinated in several ways, but the two most common processes are distillation and reverse osmosis. Distillation, the older of the two techniques, follows a protocol very similar to the natural cycling of water. Water is changed into a vapor by heating, and the condensate is collected. In reverse osmosis, salt water is filtered through a membrane that excludes salt as well as bacteria and undesirable chemicals like pesticides. Of the two methods, reverse osmosis is the least expensive.

Some of the chemicals recovered from the sea have found uses in medicine and research. In a search for more oceanic chemicals, scientists are exploring places where life abounds, such as coral reefs. Some of the most promising chemicals to date have been derived from bacteria, sponges, and sea plants. Pfu, an enzyme found in bacteria that live around geothermal vents, has provided the basis for DNA amplification, a technique that makes it possible to produce a large sample of DNA from a small one.

Minerals are mined from the ocean as construction materials and as ingredients for a variety of industrial uses. Sand and gravel are the biggest products of mineral mining and are used as ingredients in concrete and cement. Manganese, an element that can be found in metallic nodules that lie on the seafloor, is an essential component in the production of dry-cell batteries and in forming iron alloys. Metallic nodules also contain other valuable minerals such as copper, cobalt, and nickel.

Rich in the element phosphorous, the mineral phosphorite can be found on continental shelves where mineral-rich water upwells from the cold ocean floor. In the future, phosphorite mining might provide phosphorous for farmers in developing countries who need the element to fertilize their crops.

Placer deposits contain ample supplies of economically important metals, such as tin, zinc, and lead, as well as significant quantities of gold and diamond. Such deposits provide important sources of tin in Thailand. Off the coast of Alaska, placer deposits contain millions of tons of gold, which is mined by vacuuming sediments off the seafloor and sifting them for gold pieces. Diamonds are mined in a similar manner off the coast of South Africa.

Oil and gas are the two most commercially profitable resources in the ocean. Most oil is found in spongy rock layers capped with impermeable material like clay. Both oil and coal are fossil fuels, formed from the remains of dead plants and animals that were buried under sea sediments millions of years ago. Natural gas requires more heat and pressure than oil, so is usually found in deeper, older layers of rocks.

Because burning fossil fuel creates problems in the environment, cleaner alternative energy sources are being researched. Several European countries have taken significant strides to decrease their dependence on fossil fuels. Tidal power plants, like one in France, harness the energy of tides and use it to turn turbines. Wave energy plants work on a similar plan, using the energy of waves to compress air. Ocean thermal conversion energy plants heat a fluid, which vaporizes and turns the blades of a turbine. Unlike tide and wave energy plants, OTEC does not depend on the mechanical action of the ocean.

Of all the future energy sources, wind energy is the most promising. Off the coast of several European countries, wind energy towers support huge propellers. As they turn in the constant winds of the coastal regions, the propellers cause turbines to rotate, generating electricity. Cape Cod, Massachusetts, is examining plans for such a facility just off its coastline.

7

The Future of Human and Ocean Interactions

In the past, the impacts of human activities on the oceans were poorly understood, and the marine environment was treated as if it were resilient, inexhaustible, and self-sustaining. As a result, centuries of overfishing, pollution, and habitat destruction have damaged marine ecosystems, culminating in their current state of crisis.

Today, with almost half the world's population living along the coasts, marine ecosystems continue to be strained by human activities. In addition, the ever-growing population is generating newer, more global threats to seas. Ocean well-being is severely impacted by complex issues such as global warming and ozone depletion. The potential for damage from these two problems is limitless and includes devastation of food chains, loss of species, dramatic alterations in sea levels, and massive die-offs of coral reefs.

Even though past damage and current threats are extensive, the situation is not hopeless. Scientists and researchers are identifying some of the trends that have led to today's state of crisis and using the information they gather to lay down a future plan of action that will sustain marine environments. Wiser decisions about the ways people interact with the sea are now being made. The outcomes of these decisions lie in the ongoing work of politicians, scientists, policy-makers, and the public in general.

The Latest News

The U.S. Commission on Ocean Policy, a group that includes conservationists, fishermen, elected officials, naval officers, and scientists, released a preliminary report in April 2004 that may prove to be the basis for future, sustainable relationships with ocean environments. Established by President George W. Bush, the group was charged with the job of finding better ways to work with and manage ocean systems. After three years of labor, the commission generated the most comprehensive assessment of this country's marine practices in 35 years.

The recommendations of the commission are comprehensive, and to carry them out the report suggests that the federal government double its budget for ocean research (which is currently $650 million a year). The group urges the allocation of another $246 million a year for ocean education. To oversee these recommendations, the commission suggests that Congress set up a National Ocean Council.

Recommendations by the commission include the establishment of measurable, pollution-reduction goals, especially for nonpoint source pollutants such as runoff from city streets, agricultural fields, and livestock management systems. Tying in closely is the suggestion to create a form of ecosystem-based management that will monitor and limit the amount of pollution produced within well-defined marine regions.

Recognizing the value of the fishing industry, which supports thousands of individuals and businesses and contributes valuable resources to the economy, the commission warns that without drastic changes, all fishing stocks will soon be depleted. To address the problem, the commission has several recommendations, including the establishment of a fisheries management system that is based on scientific data about the health of fish stocks, regulation of fishing gear that can damage marine habitats, and establishment of plans to monitor and limit the amount of bycatch. The commission points out that the value of such programs in preserving fish stocks has already been established by the successes of earlier efforts. When limits were set on the number of striped bass that could be fished, their severely depleted populations made a dramatic comeback. After pollution was reduced along the coast of Los Angeles, fish communities there were reestablished, along with damaged kelp beds and reduced populations of seabirds. Regulation of North Atlantic swordfish fishing and protection of swordfish nurseries restored populations of these once-threatened fish.

To support the management of fisheries as well as administration and enforcement of pollution-reduction and marine educational programs, the commission wants to establish an Ocean Policy Trust Fund from money earned through the development of offshore oil and gas drilling. Currently, the U.S. Treasury Department collects about $5 billion a year in royalties and other types of payments for exploration and mining of marine fossil fuels. The commission plans to use most of this money, with the balance going toward conservation of land and water and the preservation of historically important regions.

An Eye on Today and Tomorrow

Once people learn to interact with the ocean in a harmonious way, the potential benefits are endless. In the field of research alone, the ocean holds tremendous promise. Currently, marine environments are the focus of much of the research for life-saving medicines. Of the millions of organisms that live in the ocean, only a few hundred have even been sampled as potential sources of useful drugs, and scientists feel that future sampling may produce medicines that could be used to treat devastating conditions such as malaria, cancer, and AIDS.

In the quest for new medicines, regions of the ocean that support diverse forms of life attract the most attention. Researchers looking for new molecules focus on the odd and unusual creatures, specimens such as animals that lack shells or protective armor but are avoided by predators, plants that do not have fungi or parasites living on them, and sponges that stand alone in the middle of crowded seafloor communities. These are the kinds of organisms most likely to be making biologically active compounds to protect themselves.

Already scientists have made some exciting discoveries. Tiny, saclike animals called sea squirts attach to rocks, piers, roots, and any other firm substrates. Despite their bloblike appearance, the animals are evolutionarily more closely related to humans than any of the other invertebrates. Professor Ken Rinehart of the University of Illinois has isolated a chemical from sea squirts that has life-saving potential. The chemical led to the development of an experimental drug named ecteinascidin that holds promise as a potential treatment for cancer.

Colorful marine cone snails have yielded a different kind of medicine. Cone snails produce an unusual venom that is not just made of one kind of toxin, like most venoms, but contains a mixture of dozens of nerve toxins. In nature some of the compounds in cone snail venom shock the victim, like an electric eel might do, while others cause paralysis, similar to the venom of a cobra. Pharmacologist Baldomero Olivera at the University of Utah, Salt Lake City, discovered the complex toxin and is using it to develop a new type of pain medicine he calls Prialt. This new drug may prove to be thousands of times more effective than morphine for people who suffer from chronic pain. In the body, Prialt seems to prevent pain impulses from reaching the brain by interfering with their transmission through nerves of the spinal cord.

William Fenical, director of Scripps Institution of Oceanography, California, has isolated a chemical called pseudopterosin from sea feathers, delicate cousins of sea stars. Pseudopterosin soothes swelling and may find uses in the treatment of a wide range of inflammatory conditions, from sunburn to arthritis. Fenical is also looking at a chemical from sponges that interferes with cell division in cancer cells as well as a virus-destroying chemical produced by a mold that grows on sea grass.

From his base of operations at the University of Mississippi, Dr. Mark T. Hamann has been researching the chemicals in sponges since 1993. In 2001 he found a drug that may help treat three devastating conditions: malaria, tuberculosis, and HIV infection. Called manzamine, the drug seems to stimulate the immune system, spurring the body of the person infected to fight off the disease.

The potential for life-saving medicines from the ocean is exciting, but some scientists are interested in other kinds of deep-water discoveries. The individual fibers of glass sponges are providing fascinating ideas to engineers who are working to improve fiber optic cables. The glass sponges are a group of animals that can produce thin, glasslike fibers capable of transmitting light, very similar to the high-tech fiber optic cables used in telecommunications. The naturally produced cables have several benefits over the man-made versions. Natural fiber optic cables are flexible and can be tied in knots without breaking, a practice that would snap the brittle, man-made technology. Engineers are anxious to find out how glass sponge fibers can transmit light, even though they are thin and flexible.

In a different lab, researchers have recently learned that a cousin of the sea star, the brittle star, has a unique optical system. Brittle stars are relatively simple animals that lack eyes. Recent studies have shown that each animal has multiple lenses embedded in its skin. The lenses seem to work together to form a simple eye that can pick up motion, providing a warning if a predator approaches. Researchers hope to use these lenses as models for developing improved guidance systems.

The consequences of disrespecting the ocean go further than losing a good source of raw materials; they literally bring life on Earth to the verge of extinction. The ocean is as vital a part of the Earth as the heart is of the body. Like the human body, the Earth is a single, working unit. Eact part of the unit deserves respect and care. In the past, mistakes have been made, but they can be learning experiences instead of defeats. Today people have a better sense of how their daily decisions and actions impact the whole globe. This knowledge provides them with an opportunity to work as a world community toward preserving the ocean for the benefit of future generations.

Glossary

A

algal bloom The rapid growth of cyanobacteria or algae populations that results in large mats of organisms floating in the water

ammonia A pungent, gaseous nitrogen compound that is soluble in water

anadromous fish Fish that reproduce in freshwater and spend their adult lives in the ocean

anoxic Lacking in oxygen

autotroph An organism that can capture energy to manufacture its own food from raw materials

B

barbel A fleshy projection on the head of some fish that may act as a sensory structure or function as a lure

biodiversity The number and variety of life forms that exist in a given area

biological oxygen demand (BOD) The amount of oxygen required by microorganisms to break down organic matter in water

biomagnification The accumulation of toxins in the upper levels of a food chain

brine Water that contains a lot of salt

bycatch The incidental, or noncommercial, animals caught by fishermen

C

carnivore An animal that feeds on the flesh of other animals

cartilaginous skeleton A skeleton system made of cartilage that can be found in sharks, rays, and other primitive fish

climate The long-term weather conditions in an area

coral bleaching The process in which corals expel their symbiotic algae

crude oil Unrefined petroleum

D

DDT (dichlorodiphenyltrichloroethane) A colorless insecticide that is toxic to insects and humans, and has been banned in the United States since 1972 because of its ability to persist in the environment

decomposer An organism that breaks down dead and decaying matter and releases complex molecules in the environment

detritivore Organism that feeds on dead and decaying matter

dinoflagellate A one-celled organism with two flagella for propulsion and a protective covering of cellulose

DNA Deoxyribonucleic acid, a molecule located in the nucleus of a cell that carries the genetic information responsible for running that cell

dredging Using a scoop or suction hose to remove sediment or bottom-dwelling organisms from a waterway

E

echolocation A mechanism used by some cetaceans to locate and identify objects in the ocean

emulsifier An agent that causes two liquids, such as oil and water, to mix

endangered Designation of an organism that is in danger of extinction

environment The physical and biological surroundings of an organism

enzyme Protein that regulates the speed of chemical reactions in living things

eutrophication The rapid growth of plant and animal life in waters that are rich in nutrients

exclusive economic zones (EEZs) Zones of the ocean controlled by coastal nations

extinct The designation for organisms no longer in existence

F

finning Illegal process of removing the fins from sharks

food chain The path that nutrients and energy follow as they are transferred through an ecosystem

food web Several interrelated food chains in an ecosystem

G

gastroenteritis Inflammation of the membranes of the stomach caused by pathogens or chemicals

gastropod A mollusk in the class Gastropodia, which includes snails, whelks, and abalones.

gigaton One billion tons

global warming An increase in the temperature of the Earth's surface due to trapping of heat by greenhouse gases in the atmosphere

glucose A six-carbon sugar manufactured during photosynthesis

greenway An area of undeveloped land near a waterway that is set aside to help protect the quality of water in that waterway

growth hormone A chemical that stimulates growth and development

H

habitat The place in the environment where an organism lives

harmful algal bloom (HAB) Rapid proliferation of toxin-producing microorganisms

hepatitis Inflammation of the liver caused by toxic materials or pathogens

herbivore An animal that feeds on plants

heterotroph An organism that cannot make its own food and must consume plant or animal matter to meet its body's energy needs

hydrate A compound that contains several water molecules as a part of its structure

hypothermia Low body temperature

hypoxic A condition in which oxygen levels are low

I

indicator species A species whose presence or absence indicates the condition of the environment

invertebrate An animal that lacks a backbone, such as a sponge, cnidarian, worm

L

limestone A sedimentary rock made of calcium carbonate

longline A heavy fishing line that stretches for several miles with numerous baited hooks

longshore currents Currents of water flowing parallel to long, straight beaches that carry sand and sediment from one location to another

M

macroalgae Large plants, such as seaweeds, in the marine environment

mariculture The cultivation of marine organisms for commercial purposes

microfiltration The process of filtering a solution through material that traps microscopic organisms and debris

mutation A change in DNA, the genetic material in a cell

N

nitrogen fixation The process in which some microorganisms convert atmospheric nitrogen into a form of nitrogen that producers can use

nonpoint source pollution Pollution that washes off of a variety of sources and enters waterways

O

omnivore An animal that eats both plants and animals

ozone A compound made of three oxygen atoms; in the upper atmosphere, ozone filters ultraviolet radiation

P

pathogen An organism that causes disease, such as a bacterium, virus, or fungus

PCB (polychlorinated biphenyl) One of several compounds produced from the chlorination of biphenyl that acts as an environmental pollutant

photosynthesis The process in which some organisms use the energy of the Sun to manufacture carbon compounds

phytoplankton Tiny photosynthetic organisms that float in the upper layers of the water column

point source pollution Pollution from a single, identifiable source such as a pipe

pollution Waste materials released into the air, water, or soil

productivity The rate at which energy is used to convert carbon dioxide and other raw materials into glucose

R

refined oil A product of crude oil that has been isolated by distillation

respiration A cellular process in which food is metabolized into energy for carrying out life function

rhizome The stem of a flowering plant that grows horizontally, often just under the substrate

runoff The portion of precipitation that either flows off a surface or from a subsurface

S

salinity The amount of dissolved minerals in ocean water

sargassum weed A brown seaweed of the genus *Sargassum* that lives in tropical waters of the Atlantic Ocean

schooling behavior The tendency of some types of fish to swim together for protection from predators or in search of food

sewage Liquid and solid waste from homes, businesses, and cities

sludge Semisolid material the settles from sewage

symbiotic relationship An association between two different kinds of organisms that usually benefits both

T

thermophiles Organisms that require high temperatures for normal development

threatened A designation to indicate an organism whose existence is likely to become endangered

transgenic Relating to the change of an organism's DNA by the transfer of genes from another organism

turbidity The cloudiness of a solution due to suspended particles

U

ultraviolet light Electromagnetic energy whose wavelength is shorter than the wavelength of visible light

upwelling The process in which cold, nutrient-laden deepwater is moved to the surface by wind and currents

V

vulnerable A designation to indicate an organism whose existence is likely to become threatened

W

watershed The region of land draining into a body of water

Z

zooplankton Tiny, animal-like organisms that float in the upper layers of the water column

Further Reading and Web Sites

Books

Banister, Keith, and Andrew Campbell. *The Encyclopedia of Aquatic Life*. New York: Facts On File, 1985. Well written and beautifully illustrated book on all aspects of the ocean and its organisms.

Davis, Richard A. *Oceanography, An Introduction to the Marine Environment*. Dubuque, Iowa: Wm. C. Brown Publishers, 1991. A text that helps students become familiar with, and appreciate, the world's oceans.

Dean, Cornelia. *Against the Tide*. New York: Columbia University Press, 1999. An analysis of the impact of humans and nature on the ever-changing beaches.

Garrison, Tom. *Oceanography*. New York: Wadsworth Publishing Company, 1996. An interdisciplinary examination of the ocean for beginning marine science students.

Karleskint, George, Jr. *Introduction to Marine Biology*. Belmont, Calif.: Brooks/Cole-Thompson Learning, 1998. An enjoyable text on marine organisms and their relationships with one another and with their physical environments.

McCutcheon, Scott, and Bobbi McCutcheon. *The Facts On File Marine Science Handbook*. New York: Facts On File, 2003. An excellent resource that includes information on marine physical factors and living things as well as people who have been important in ocean studies.

Nowak, Ronald M. *Walker's Marine Mammals of the World*. Baltimore: Johns Hopkins University Press, 2003. An overview on the anatomy, taxonomy, and natural history of the marine mammals.

Pinet, Paul R. *Invitation to Oceanography*. Sudbury, Mass.: Jones and Bartlett Publishers, 2000. Includes explanations of the causes and effects of tides and currents, as well as the origins of ocean habitats.

Prager, Ellen J. *The Sea*. New York: McGraw-Hill, 2000. An evolutionary view of life in the Earth's oceans.

Reeves, Randall R., Brent S. Steward, Phillip J. Clapham, and James A. Powell. *Guide to Marine Mammals of the World*. New York: Alfred A. Knopf, 2002. An encyclopedic work on sea mammals, accompanied by gorgeous color plates.

Sverdrup, Keith A., Alyn C. Duxbury, and Alison B. Duxbury. *An Introduction to the World's Oceans*. New York: McGraw-Hill, 2003. A comprehensive text on all aspects of the physical ocean, including the seafloor and the ocean's physical properties.

Thorne-Miller, Boyce, and John G Catena. *The Living Ocean*. Washington, D.C.: Friends of the Earth, 1991. A study of the loss of diversity in ocean habitats.

Waller, Geoffrey. *SeaLife, A Complete Guide to the Marine Environment*. Washington, D.C.: Smithsonian Institution Press, 1996. A text that describes the astonishing diversity of organisms in the sea.

Web Sites

Bird, Jonathon. "Adaptations for Survival in the Sea." Oceanic Research Group, 1996. Available online. URL: http://www.oceanicresearch.org/adapspt.html. Accessed March 19, 2004. A summary and review of the educational film of the same name that describes and illustrates some of the adaptations that animals have for life in salt water.

Blue Ocean. Available online. URL: http://www.blueoceansociety.org. Accessed January 9, 2005. Provides marine information to the public in hopes of inspiring more people to help protect marine life.

Buchheim, Jason. "A Quick Course in Ichthyology, Odyssey Expeditions." Available online. URL: http://www.marinebiology.org/fish.htm. Accessed January 4, 2004. A detailed explanation of fish physiology.

Gulf of Maine Research Institute. Available online. URL: http://www.gma.org/about_GMA/default.asp. Accessed January 2, 2004. A comprehensive and up-to-date research site on all forms of marine life.

"Habitat Guides from eNature." Available online. URL: http://www.enature.com/habitats/show_sublifezone.asp?sublifezoneID=60#Anchor-habitat-49575. Accessed November 21, 2003. A Web site with young people in mind that provides comprehensive information on habitats, organisms, and physical ocean factors.

Huber, Brian T. "Climate Change Records from the Oceans: Fossil Foraminifera," Calypso Log, Smithsonian National Museum of Natural History, June 1993. Available online. URL: http://www.nmnh.si.edu/paleo/marine/foraminifera.htm. Accessed December 30, 2003. A concise look at the natural history of foraminifera.

King County's Marine Waters. Natural Resources and Parks, Water and Land Resources Divisions. Available online. URL: http://splash.metrokc.gov/wlr/waterres/marine/index.htm. Accessed December 2, 2003. A terrific Web site on all aspects of the ocean, emphasizing the organisms that live there.

Mapes, Jennifer. "U.N. Scientists Warn of Catastrophic Climate Changes." National Geographic News, February 6, 2001. Available online. URL: http://news.nationalgeographic.com/news/2001/02/0206_climate1.html.

Accessed January 9, 2005. A first-rate overview of the current data and consequences of global warming.

Marine Conservation Biology Institute. Available online. URL: http://www.mcbi.org. Accessed January 9, 2005. A resource of news items on issues that relate to marine conservancy.

National Oceanic and Atmospheric Administration (NOAA). Available online. URL: http://www.noaa.gov. Accessed January 9, 2005. A top-notch resource for news, research, diagrams, and photographs relating to the oceans, coasts, weather, climate, and research.

Ocean.com. Available online: http://www.ocean.com/Conservation. Accessed January 9, 2005. An organization that provides information from around the world on ocean news, education, conservation, and entertainment.

Pew Ocean Commission. Available online. URL: http://www.pewoceans.org. Accessed January 9, 2005. This Web site contains America's Living Ocean, the commission's report on the current condition of the oceans and its recommendations for the oceans' future.

Sierra Club. Available online. URL: http://www.sierraclub.org/policy/conservation/marine.asp. Accessed January 9, 2005. A source of information on all conservation topics, including the oceans, with the goal of teaching people to protect the wild places on Earth.

"Spinner Dolphin," Defenders of Wildlife. Available online. URL: http://www.kidsplanet.org/factsheets/spinnerdolphin.html. Accessed February 20, 2004. An excellent Web site suitable for both children and young adults that describes various species of marine animals.

U.S. Fish and Wildlife Service. Available online. URL: http://www.fws.gov. Accessed January 9, 2005. A federal conservation organization that covers a wide range of topics, including fisheries, endangered animals, the condition of the oceans, and conservation news.

"Why Care About Reefs?" REN Reef Education Network, Environment Australia, 2001. Available online. URL: http://www.reef.edu.au. Accessed February 2, 2004. A superb Web site dedicated to the organisms on and the health of the coral reefs.

Index

Note: *Italic* page numbers indicate illustrations.
C indicates color insert pages.

F

G

H

I

J

K

L

M

N

O

P

R

S

T

U

W

Z